DEATH ON THE RIMROCK

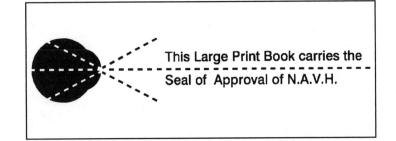

This Large Print Book carries the
Seal of Approval of N.A.V.H.

DEATH ON THE RIMROCK

BRADFORD SCOTT

WHEELER PUBLISHING
A part of Gale, Cengage Learning

GALE
CENGAGE Learning

Detroit • New York • San Francisco • New Haven, Conn • Waterville, Maine • London

GALE
CENGAGE Learning

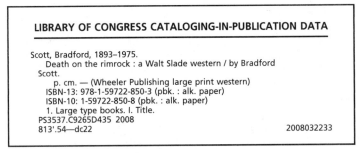

LIBRARY OF CONGRESS CATALOGING-IN-PUBLICATION DATA

Scott, Bradford, 1893–1975.
  Death on the rimrock : a Walt Slade western / by Bradford
Scott.
    p. cm. — (Wheeler Publishing large print western)
    ISBN-13: 978-1-59722-850-3 (pbk. : alk. paper)
    ISBN-10: 1-59722-850-8 (pbk. : alk. paper)
    1. Large type books. I. Title.
PS3537.C9265D435 2008
813'.54—dc22   2008032233

Published in 2008 by arrangement with Golden West Literary Agency.

3 0073 00302 8330

Printed in the United States of America
1 2 3 4 5 6 7 12 11 10 09 08

DEATH ON THE RIMROCK

ONE

The tall man with the heavy black beard rode up to the Cross W ranch house yard, his horse's hoofs making but a whisper of sound on the thick grass. Because of the beard that grew high on his cheeks, little of his features could be seen save the glint of eyes under his low-drawn hat brim.

In the shade of a big tree he drew rein and swept his surroundings with a quick glance.

To all appearances, the place was deserted. The ranch house door stood open. So did the bunkhouse door. No sound broke the stillness.

Deserted? Not quite. At the far edge of the yard a girl knelt beside a flower bed, busy with a trowel and a collection of bulbs. The sun struck reddish glints in her curly dark hair.

The bearded man dismounted, dropped the split reins to the ground and strode across the yard. So quiet were his lithe steps that the first inkling the kneeling girl had of his presence was two long and powerful arms clasping her, pinning her own arms to her sides, holding her helpless. She caught a glimpse of the black beard as he jerked her to her feet. A scream welled in her throat, but a hand clamped over her mouth, stifling it. He draped her across an arm, lifted her and held her with her feet hanging on one side, her head on the other, struggling, but to no avail. He turned and strode purposefully toward his horse.

But as he reached the ranch house porch, he abruptly turned at right angles, mounted the steps and entered the ranch house. In the luxuriously furnished living room he dropped her to her feet and whirled her around to face him.

Her wide, darkly blue eyes were filled with terror, but as they rested on the bearded face, their expression changed to one of astonished gladness.

"Walt!" she gasped.

The eyes changed again. Now their expression was distinctly a glare.

"You devil!" she stormed. "Of all the things to do! You scared me out of my wits."

Ranger Walt Slade, named by the Mexican *peones* of the Rio Grande river villages, *El*

Halcon — The Hawk — shook with laughter.

"Sort of evened up for some of the capers you've pulled on me," he said. "Like over at Angelo, the silver town, where you inveigled Sheriff Miller and Rimrock Rawlins, the saloon owner, into letting you show up on the dance floor, with me not knowing you were anywhere within a hundred miles."

Miss Mary Merril giggled. "It was delicious to see your face when I pranced out of the dressing room in my very short, spangled skirt and my very low neckline devoid of spangles."

"Yes," he retorted, "and it was delicious to see your face a minute ago, when you thought the bearded villain had you in his clutches."

"You devil!" she repeated, but this time with a lilting note to her soft voice as she snuggled close in his arms. "You'd drive any woman crazy."

"You've said that before," he pointed out.

"Yes, but that was different," she said. "I don't want any repeat performances of this one. But oh, darling, I am glad to see you; didn't expect you to get down this way so soon. You're neglecting your other women."

"What other women!" he answered indignantly, with an unsuccessful attempt at innocence.

"Oh, never mind," she said. "But why the whiskers? Not that they aren't becoming; remind me of a painting of Jean LaFitte, the Gulf pirate, I once saw; and the resemblance is more than skin, or whiskers deep. Quite a bit in common, you two. Why'd you grow 'em?"

"I was up close to the Panhandle and over by the New Mexico line when I got word from Captain McNelty that Sheriff Crane was very anxious to see me down here," Slade explained. "I've been riding steadily for nearly a week and didn't have time to shave, and the darn things grow fast. Figured I'd do better riding rather than to take the round-about way by the railroad, with accommodations to be provided for my horse, and everything. So here I am."

"And it's wonderful to have you, whiskers and all," she said. "And Uncle John will be glad to see you, too."

"I met Webb out on the range," Slade replied. "He was riding to inspect a water-hole but said he would be along shortly. He told me you were here alone, that everybody else had ridden to Sanderson, today being payday for the spreads and the railroad. Glad you weren't in the house or I wouldn't have had the chance to play my little joke."

"Joke! You have such a quaint sense of

humor. Frighten a girl out of her — her equilibrium! But gracious, you must be hungry. I'll have you coffee and something to eat in a jiffy. Come on out to the kitchen with me."

"Okay, and thanks," he answered. "Then I'll have to head for town and a word with Tom Crane."

"Oh, the sheriff can wait a little longer," she said. "Incidentally, Uncle John and I plan to ride to Sanderson a little later. See you there, of course. Suppose you'll be staying at the Regan House, as usual?"

"Yes, and you?" he said smilingly. Miss Merril tossed her shining curls.

"You know very well Uncle John and I always stop there," she said.

"Oh, come to think of it, you do, or so I seem to remember," he replied.

"Beast!" she retorted, and headed for the kitchen.

"I'll take care of my horse and then join you," Slade called after her.

"And how is dear old Shadow?" she asked over her shoulder.

"Fine as frog hair," Slade answered. "All ready to take somebody's arm off."

"Just like he was ready to make a lunch off mine when I reached for him before you'd properly introduced me. He's sure a

11

one-man horse, all right. Don't be long, dear, everything will soon be ready."

Thoroughly familiar with the Cross W layout, Slade led Shadow, his magnificent black horse, to the barn and removed the rig. He put oats in a manger, water handy, and returned to the kitchen, where his coffee and snack were ready and waiting.

"Mary," he said as they sat together at the table, "why is Tom Crane so anxious to see me?"

"Walt," the girl replied, "terrible things have been happening hereabouts of late, even worse than when you were here before. After you cleaned out Juan Covello and his bunch, and Crater Moral, it was quiet and peaceful, comparatively speaking, but of late outlawry has been rampant — robberies, killings, burglaries. Even a couple of our carts looted, something that never happened before. Sheriff Crane admits he isn't able to cope with the situation, so he wrote Captain McNelty for help. I'm afraid it is going to mean difficulty and danger for you, but to you that's an old story, and I'm sure glad Captain Jim decided to send you, even though Sheriff Crane figures he needs a whole troop of Rangers to straighten things out. Guess he'll be satisfied with one, so long as that one is you."

12

"Hope he won't be disappointed," Slade returned cheerfully. "Anyhow, I'll do my best."

"Which will be enough," Mary declared with conviction.

"You say two of your carts were looted," Slade remarked. "That was unusual."

Mary Merril, he knew, was half owner of the lucrative carting business run by her uncle, John Webb, and one Pancho Arista. Incidentally, she was half owner of Webb's big ranch.

"Yes, of a valuable shipment," she replied to his indirect question. "We didn't mind the loss so much, although it was considerable, we can take it, but —" she shuddered — "but the night watchman was found dead, knife in his back. The guards have been tripled since that."

"I see," Slade said thoughtfully. "Sanderson is an up and coming town, what with the railroad shops and yards and more business all the time, and naturally attracts questionable characters from the Big Bend country to the southwest and from elsewhere. Well, we'll see."

He glanced out the window as his amazingly keen hearing caught the whisper of hoofs on the heavy grass.

"Here comes Uncle John, now," he said.

13

"Glad he made it before I left."

A few minutes later, John Webb entered the kitchen. He was a huge man with gray-streaked hair, hot blue eyes and craggy features.

"Hello!" he greeted. "So you found her, eh?"

"Yes, he found me," Mary said. "Scared me half to death. Let me tell you about it."

As the story progressed in detail, old John roared with laughter.

"So!" he chuckled. "Okay for you to play outlandish pranks on folks, but when the shoe's on the other foot it sorta pinches. Good for him! Maybe she'll tone down a bit now," he added to Slade.

"I doubt it," the Ranger replied morosely. "I expect right now she's figuring a way to get even."

"Wouldn't be surprised," Webb agreed. "Suppose you're heading for town?"

"Yes, I'm leaving now," Slade replied. "It's past noon and I'd like to make it well before dark, so I can get a room and shave and clean up a bit."

"Why spoil such a nice crop of whiskers?" Webb said.

"The darn things itch," Slade explained.

"Always do when they're brand new, but stop after a bit," Webb predicted. "Okay,

Mary and I will be along after a while. I hanker for a bite to eat first. Gotta keep an eye on my young hellions. When they're in town with money burnin' holes in their pockets, they're liable to get mixed up in something if I don't. Meet you at Hardrock Hogan's Branding Pen, as he calls that rumhole he runs."

Mary accompanied Slade to the barn for a word with Shadow.

"See you later, dear," she said. "I hope you won't go gallivanting off somewhere."

"I sure hope so, too," he replied pointedly, and with a heartiness that caused her to blush.

As they watched him ride away, old John thought, justly, what a fine looking young man he was.

Walt Slade was very tall, more than six feet, and the breadth of his shoulders and the depth of his chest matched his height. His face was as arresting as his splendid form. A rather wide mouth, grin-quirked at the corners, relieved somewhat the tinge of fierceness evinced by the prominent hawk nose above and the powerful jaw and chin beneath. His hair was thick and crisp, and so black a blue shadow seemed to lie upon it at times.

The sternly handsome countenance was

marked by long, black-lashed eyes of very pale gray, cold reckless eyes, in the clear depths of which little devils of laughter always seemed to lurk. That is, when laughter was in order. Otherwise they could leap to the front and be anything but laughing. Then those eyes became "the terrible eyes of El Halcon," before which armed men had been known to cringe.

Slade wore with careless grace the homely garb of the range land — Levi's, the bibless overalls favored by cowhands, soft blue shirt with vivid neckerchief looped at the throat, well scuffed half-boots of softly tanned leather, and the broad-brimmed "J.B.", the rainshed of the plains.

Around his lean, sinewy waist were double cartridge belts, from the carefully worked and oiled cut-out holsters of which protruded the plain black butts of heavy guns. And from the butts of those big Colts, his slender, muscular hands seemed never far away.

Two

After some miles of steady riding, Slade reached the mouth of Echo Canyon, a narrow, gloomy, brush-grown gorge that was the most direct route through the hills to

16

the Sanderson trail. Entering the canyon, he slackened Shadow's gait a bit, for the floor of the gorge was rough and stony, the going none too good.

He reached a point, about midway through, where the canyon curved and the visibility ahead was cut to less than fifty yards. He rode warily, watching the movements of birds on the wing, and of little animals in the brush, for the sinister bore had an evil history.

Abruptly he raised his head in an attitude of listening.

"Horses coming, coming fast, two of them I'd say," he remarked to Shadow. "Gents 'pear to be in a hurry. Okay, we'll give them room to pass."

He edged the tall black close to the brush and drew rein, listening to the loudening beat of hoofs.

Around the bend bulged two riders, going like the wind. They gave a startled yelp as they sighted the tall form of El Halcon, jerked their mounts to a halt and went for the guns at their waists.

They were good, darn good, their reach but a blur of motion, but not good enough to swap lead with "the fastest gunhand in the whole Southwest." Slade drew and shot with both hands before the pair could line sights. Weaving, ducking, dodging, he answered the pair shot for shot.

Moments later, one shirt sleeve shot to ribbons, a red streak burned along his cheek just above the line of beard, Slade lowered his smoking Colts and gazed at the two motionless forms lying in the dust of the trail. Their horses had bolted back a little ways and stood blowing and snorting.

"Nice little reception committee," he said to Shadow. "Section 'pears to be running true to form. Looks like — say! Here come some more! Five or six this time. Guess we'd better get in the clear till we know what's what. Into the brush with you!"

Swiftly he maneuvered the horse into the growth and sat where he could view the trail through a leafy fringe, himself well out of sight.

Louder and louder sounded the multiple beat of hoofs. Around the bend surged five horsemen. They uttered shouts of astonishment, pulled their horses to a slithering halt and for a moment sat staring in bewilderment. Then they dismounted, swearing and exclaiming. Slade got a good view of their faces and grinned. He waited until they were clustered around the two bodies, babbling unanswerable questions at each other. Then he called,

"Just like a cow's tail, always behind!"

The group jumped five feet in the air, a foot to each member, and whirled toward the sound of his voice, clutching at their weapons.

"What the blankety-blank-blank!" bawled a voice. "Who the devil are you? Come outa there and show yourself before we smoke you out."

"Gladly," Slade replied, and spoke to Shadow. "How are you, Tom?"

Sheriff Tom Crane, a grizzled veteran, cut loose with an explosive oath. Then, as El Halcon emerged from the growth, he gave a joyous whoop,

"Slade! where the devil did you come from? Always Johnny-on-the-spot at just the right time! What the blankety-blank happened here? Did those two sidewinders try to gun you?"

"Appeared that was what they had in mind," Slade replied composedly. "Didn't work."

"Sorta looks that way," Sheriff Crane agreed dryly. Slade assumed a more sober mien.

"Who and what were they?" he asked.

"A couple of blasted owlhoots," the sheriff growled. "Held up a saloon in Sanderson, shot a bartender, not too bad. We got a

19

lucky break. Were just ridin' into town from over toward Langtry, where some trouble had been reported. I figured the devils would make for this crack and we hightailed after them. Sighted them just as they were turning into the canyon. Was scairt they'd give us the slip, for when they saw us they speeded up and were pulling away from us; our horses had already covered quite a few miles and were sorta fagged. Sure glad you happened along to lend us a hand."

"I didn't have much choice in the matter," Slade replied. "They were going for their irons and they were darned fast. I didn't have time to pick my shots; just had to cut loose at the thickest part."

"Darned good thing you didn't take chances," Crane said. "They were killers."

"Have to admit it looked that way," Slade agreed. "So you have another bunch working the section, eh?"

"So it 'pears," the sheriff admitted wearily. He turned to his followers, two of whom were specials who were regarding Slade in a puzzled fashion, the other two being his regular deputies, who knew Slade well.

"Walt," he said, "I want you to know a couple of work dodgers we brought along for company. Boys, guess you've both heard of El Halcon, the notorious owlhoot too

20

smart to get caught. Well, that's him. He's been my deputy for quite a while; I keep him with me down here to keep him outa trouble."

The two specials shook hands, diffidently, and stared, almost in awe, at the man whose exploits, some considered questionable, in certain quarters, were fast becoming legend throughout the Southwest. Crane chuckled and supplied the names of the two.

"Well, guess we might as well collect the carcasses and head for town," he said. "Be getting along toward dark by the time we make it."

"Take a look in the saddle pouches," Slade suggested. "May find the saloon keeper's money in them."

The outlaws' horses, which had quieted and were nibbling at grass, were easily caught. Examination of the pouches justified Slade's prediction.

"Yep, it's here," said Crane. "Every peso, I'd say. This sure turned out a heap better'n I hoped for, thanks to you. Just a minute, let's see what's in the horned toads' pockets.

"Say!" he exclaimed a few minutes later, "we're makin' a nice profit. A lot more dinero here than planting the devils will cost. And those cayuses are first rate critters and should bring a good price. Just let you stick around a while and the county will get rich."

Slade laughed and helped secure the bodies to the saddles they had forked in life. The posse got under way, taking it easy, for their horses had had a hard day.

The sunset was flaming its splendor when they reached the outskirts of Sanderson, the railroad town, where things were already quite lively, the payday just getting under way.

Sanderson sits in a deep canyon, one wall of which rises over the main street. It still was a wild frontier town. Outlaws roamed the mountains and canyons of the Big Bend country to the southwest. Among other questionable practices, they trafficked in "wet" herds stolen in Mexico and driven across the Rio Grande, often at the old Comanche Crossing deep in the Big Bend.

They varied this activity by running wide-looped Texas cows to ready buyers across the great river in Mexico. So the traffic paid both going and coming. Sanderson was the logical place to spend their ill gotten gains.

Yes, Sanderson was bad enough even before the coming of the railroad brought more citizens, some of them of dubious characteristics, more saloons, and more trouble.

The town had a colorful history. Many

famous, or notorious personages lived there at one time or another, including Judge Roy "Law West of the Pecos" Bean, who after an adventurous life as a pony express rider and freighter, founded the town of Vingaroon, east of Sanderson, which he renamed Langtry, after the actress Lily Langtry, the "Jersey Lily" whom he persuaded to visit the town.

After being elected Justice of the Peace, he held court with a law book in one hand and a six-shooter in the other.

Also of Sanderson were the Regan brothers, the searchers for the Lost Negro Mine. They had sent a colored man of their employ to round up some stray horses. Instead of horses, he returned with a knapsack and his pockets full of rocks. The angered Regans walloped him a couple for his disobedience and chased him out of camp. A little later, to their astonishment and dismay, they realized that the "rocks" were rich gold ore. They spent a fortune trying to locate the colored man, and never did. None of the many searchers that followed ever re-discovered the fabulous gold-bearing ledge, but it undoubtedly exists somewhere in the vicinity of Sanderson.

Sanderson became a repair and crew change division on the Southern Pacific

Railroad with large shops and yards, and in consequence, Sanderson boomed, attracting more gentlemen the more sober citizens felt they could well do without.

THREE

The posse and its grim burden created more than a little excitement as it threaded its way through the narrow streets to the sheriff's office and occasioned volleys of questions on the part of those who quickly thronged the office.

Sheriff Crane did the answering, and where Walt Slade was concerned, the account lost nothing in the telling. Slade was the subject of admiration and praise, which he felt he could have well done without. However, he knew there was no stopping Tom Crane when he really got going. Finally he managed to create a diversion.

"Do you think that bartender who was shot is in a condition to talk?" he asked.

"Sure he is," several voices replied. "Doc Cooper tied up the hole in his arm and he's settin' in the saloon cussin' and gettin' drunk. Figure he's havin' the time of his life."

"Then I expect he would come here for a look at the bodies," Slade suggested. "Might be able to tell us something of value."

"That's a notion," Crane agreed and dispatched the two specials to tie onto the barkeep before he reached a condition in which he would be unable to walk, which Slade thought would likely happen.

However, when he arrived, quite mellow but still able to navigate, he had a surprise for the law enforcement officers.

"Are those the two hellions who held you up and shot you?" Crane asked.

"Couldn't say," replied the drink juggler.

"No? Why not?"

"Because the devils I busted in on cleanin' the safe of a week's take had black rags tied over their faces.

"Wait a minute though," he added as the sheriff began to swear. "I saw both of those horned toads on the floor there before. They were in the Hog Wallow, the saloon, just a little while before the joint was held up and I got plugged. Wasn't the first time, either. Were there the night before. I remember 'em, all right, especially the short one because of that reddish birth mark on his cheek. A notion you got the right pair, Sheriff."

"Seein' as the Hog Wallow dinero is in their saddle pouches, I reckon we did," Crane agreed. "Okay, Zack, much obliged for coming in. Go back and finish your chore of getting ossified; 'spect it'll be the best thing for you."

"Doc rec-hic-mended it," replied Zack. "Gotta obey doctor's ordesh."

"Go with him, boys, and prop him up with something," Crane told the specials.

Now the bartender had started the ball rolling, several more gents expressed the opinion that they had seen the pair somewhere around town. Slade was dubious as to how much credence was to be put in their statements. Could be just power of suggestion working, especially as the informants were vague as to just when or where they had noticed the two outlaws.

"Okay, out, the lot of you," ordered the sheriff. "Come back later, if you're of a mind to. Right now we hanker for a surroundin'. Chasin' owlhoots always makes me hungry."

After the last straggler had been shooed out and the two deputies dispatched to care for the horses, except Shadow, who was left right where he was until Slade accompanied him to his stable, Crane shut and locked the door and turned to the Ranger.

"Well, what do you think?" he asked.

"Oh, there's no doubt but they were the pair who pulled the robbery," Slade replied.

26

"The fact that they were masked is interesting, seeming to indicate either that they had been hanging around town or expected to return after making their get-away. Removed the masks once they were out of town. Must have tossed them away; certainly are not on their persons. Smart operators, all right."

"And if it wasn't for you, they would have gotten away with it," growled the sheriff.

"Yes, smooth operators," Slade repeated. "They were hanging around, of course, to get the low down on the place, and evidently did. I remember the Hog Wallow, a carelessly run place. A door leading from the back room onto an alley. Wouldn't be surprised if that door was unlocked half the time, and safe open."

"That's right," agreed the sheriff. "Cruikshanks, the owner, drinks so much of the likker there ain't much left for the customers. Reckon he don't give a darn how the place is run; he's well heeled, made his pile in the freighting business, is still in it to an extent, and runs that rumhole just as a sort of pastime; gives him a place to loaf and drink in. You figure those two were all of the bunch?"

"I very much doubt it," Slade replied. "Strike me as the sort that would be affiliated with others of the same brand. Guesswork on my part, of course, but I've a notion I'm right."

"You usually are," grunted Crane. "And I figure just two couldn't have by themselves pulled all the devilishness that's been cutting loose hereabouts of late. Okay, let's put up your nag and amble over to Hardrock Hogan's Branding Pen for a snort and something to eat. Hardrock will be plumb glad to see you, and so will a lot of other folks."

"And some won't be," he added sententiously.

The elderly Mexican who ran the livery stable was one of those greatly pleased by El Halcon's return. He bowed low, shook hands diffidently. They exchanged greetings in Spanish, which delighted the old fellow. Slade left Shadow in his care, knowing the big black would receive the very best treatment.

"Now for the Regan House and a room, where I'll stow my saddle pouches," he said. "After we eat, I want to shave and clean up a bit."

"Whiskers look fine," said Crane. "I'd grow some, only folks would take me for Santa Claus; mine are snow white."

The chore of registering for a room cared for, they repaired to the Branding Pen,

28

where Hardrock Hogan, the owner, also had a warm greeting for Slade. The place was crowded, but Hardrock led them to a vacant table near the dance floor.

"When I heard you were in town, I kept it open for you, Mr. Slade," he said. "It was always your favorite when you were here before."

It was. For from it, Slade had a view of the swinging doors and the windows, and a good portion of the big room as reflected in the back-bar mirror.

Hardrock Hogan was big and burly and not exactly a prepossessing person at first glance, but a square shooter from his underslung jaw, his wide, almost reptilian mouth and crooked nose to his narrowed eyes and his bristling red hair. His place was run strictly on the up-and-up, including drinks, games, and dance floor girls. No one had to fear mistreatment or being taken advantage of in the Branding Pen.

However, it was not a good place in which to start trouble; Hardrock had a couple of floor men about the same size as himself, and when the three of them gently remonstrated with would-be belligerents, all the fight was quickly taken out of the gentlemen in question.

Hardrock had been a prospector —

whence his nickname — had made a good strike and invested it in the Branding Pen, which soon became more of a gold mine than the ledges he discovered.

"Gotta tell the cook who's here, so he can stir up something special," Hardrock said, and headed for the kitchen, out the door of which another old Mexican stuck his head a moment later and waved to Slade, who returned the greeting.

"With you here, eatin' is plumb an event," chuckled Crane. "You got the kitchen force in your vest pocket."

"Only I'm not wearing a vest," Slade returned smilingly.

"Just the same as you were," the sheriff replied cheerfully. Which Slade did not try to unscramble.

Quite a few of those present showed an inclination to praise and congratulate Slade, the deputies and specials having spread the word of what happened in Echo Canyon, but Hardrock shooed everybody away so the two law enforcement officers could enjoy their dinner in peace.

When the food arrived, it was all Sheriff Crane predicted it would be and for a while conversation languished. Finally the sheriff pushed back his empty plate with a contented sigh, ordered a snort and hauled out his pipe. Slade ordered more coffee and rolled a cigarette.

As he smoked, Slade studied the room and its occupants. The Branding Pen was a typical frontier town saloon of the better sort, with its long and shining bar, its spotlessly clean lunch counter, its table for leisurely diners, others for games, two roulette wheels and a faro bank. There was a fairly commodious dance floor, now jam-packed, and a really good Mexican orchestra.

The patrons were a varied lot. There were railroaders, cowhands — plenty of both — shop keepers, clerical workers, and some others not so easily catalogued, although they, for the most part, dressed as cowhands. Also, quite a number of Mexicans, well dressed, well-behaved young fellows, the majority of whom, Slade rightly deduced, were employees of the big and lucrative carting train owned by Mary Merril, John Webb, and Pancho Arista.

Those present of whose real status Slade was not sure were the ones that interested him most, and whom he studied most intensely, watching gestures and facial expressions, his extraordinarily keen ears catching occasional scraps of conversation. There was no better place in the West, he knew, for picking up information than a saloon. A too liberal helping of redeye causing men to raise their voices and sometimes become a mite careless as to what they said. If some of the outlaw bunch operating in the section happened to be among those at the bar or tables, a chance remark might prove valuable; it had happened in the past.

Pinching out his cigarette, Slade stood up. "I'm going over to the hotel to clean up a bit," he said. "If John Webb and Mary come in while I'm gone, tell them I'll be back shortly."

"Okay," replied Crane. "Watch your step. Got a notion you ain't overly popular in certain quarters about now. Somebody might be out to even up for those two sidewinders you did in."

"Hope so," Slade said carelessly. "I sure haven't the slightest notion where to look for them; might help if they come looking for me."

The sheriff gave a disgusted snort and ordered another drink.

In his room, Slade shaved, bathed and donned a clean shirt and overalls. Deciding he looked fairly presentable, he locked the door and descended the stairs.

Outside, he hesitated. He knew the specials and Charley and Bert, the sheriff's deputies, were circulating through the town on the lookout for possible trouble; Sanderson being not exactly tame on payday nights. He concluded to emulate their example for a while.

The streets, especially Main Street, were crowded with a gay and colorful throng and everybody appeared to be having a good time. Music, laughter, and a babble of voices boiled over the swinging doors of the saloons. On the dance floors, boots thumped and high heels clicked. Altogether, it was a night to quicken the pulses, and El Halcon enjoyed his stroll.

The weather had apparently decided to cooperate, for the air was pleasantly cool with no wind. Overhead the bonfire stars of Texas bloomed in their silver beauty. East, south and west were mountains, some of them near, their crests glowing in the starlight, their mighty chests and shoulders robed in purple shadow. With the sinister wasteland that was the Big Bend rolling on and on to the mighty flood of the Rio Grande. Slade thrilled to its austere beauty and grandeur. The "rock" on which the tide of Spanish conquest split, to flow northward on either side, leaving it as it was since the days of the Dawn Men and before. Only the hardiest of men and women braved savage men, savage beasts, and the dumb, imponderable forces of Nature to establish homes amid its wild solitude and ever present threat. The Big Bend! Texas!

Noise and hilarity were all Slade encountered as he wandered about. There was the usual rough horseplay and cutting up, with the squeals of dance floor girls who had slipped out for a breath of fresh air vying with the guffaws of their male companions. Otherwise, everything appeared peaceful enough.

He paused at a corner for a moment, then decided to visit the Hog Wallow, where the holdup occurred, which was near the railroad yards and no great distance from the Branding Pen. So he turned the corner and moseyed on.

He was just approaching the swinging doors of the rather dingy looking saloon, when from inside came a burst of profanity and angry shouts. He bulged through the doors hurriedly. Sounded like a real ruckus had cut loose.

Inside, he shot a quick glance around, then bounded forward. On the floor lay a man Slade recognized as Bert Estes, the deputy sheriff. A big fellow with a bad-tempered face was just drawing back a boot, apparently intending to kick the prone deputy in the head. The next instant, a fist, like the slim, steely face of a sledgehammer, crashed against his jaw and laid him on the floor beside the deputy, who was striving to rise.

The fellow's companions, a half dozen of them, turned on Slade with angry yelps, and met a barrage of fists left and right that put two more on the floor and sent the others reeling and staggering. One raised a mug to throw at Slade, but a gent with one arm in a sling brought a bottle crashing down on his head. Glass and whiskey flew in every direction, but the recipient of the favor didn't mind; he was sound asleep on the sawdust.

Suddenly Slade slithered sideways; the big man on the floor, his chin and throat crimsoned from a split lip, had jerked a gun.

There was a crash of a shot. The gun, one butt plate knocked off by the Ranger's bullet, clattered halfway across the room. Its owner gave a howl of pain and clutched his blood spurting hand.

FOUR

That stopped the fighting, for now Slade had a gun in each hand, one wisping smoke. And back of those rock-steady Colts that menaced the group, were the pale, cold, terrible eyes of El Halcon. And beside him was Deputy Bert Estes, a cocked gun also ready for business.

"All right, what was it all about?" Slade asked him.

"They were startin' a row and I was trying to quiet them down and somebody threw a punch at me," Estes replied. "I stepped back and onto a wet spot and slipped and fell down. Fletch Bartlett there was going to kick me in the face."

"I wasn't!" came an indignant denial from the floor. "I was just tryin' to shove you out of the way."

Slade swept the room with a glance, centered it for an instant on the bottle-whacked gentleman, who was thrashing about and rolling his head with returning consciousness. He holstered his guns and spoke to Bartlett, who was mumbling cuss words over his split lip and cherishing his bullet-creased hand.

"Get on your feet and I'll take care of your hand," Slade told him. "You're not badly hurt. Zack," he said to the wounded bartender, who had been obeying the doctor's orders and was somewhat sobered by the shindig, "see if you can find something that will do for a bandage."

"Got everything in the back room," Zack replied. "We need 'em."

"I imagine you do," Slade observed dryly as Zack hurried away to return shortly with the medical kit, with which Slade soon had the injured hand smeared with a soothing salve and padded and bandaged.

"Feller, you're all right," said Bartlett. "I'm sorry for going off half cocked like I did, but my mouth hurt."

"Not a wise thing to do," Slade answered. "I might have missed — a little to the right."

Bartlett got it, and shivered. Abruptly Slade smiled, the flashing white smile of El Halcon that men, and women, found irresistible. Bartlett grinned sheepishly in reply.

"Fletch," said Zack, the barkeep, "the only reason you're alive is that Mr. Slade didn't hanker to kill you. Tried to swap draws with El Halcon, eh? With the fastest gunhand in the whole blankety-blank Southwest!"

Fletcher Bartlett stared at Slade, his jaw dropping. Then he snapped it shut and said,

"Feller, I don't care what you are or where you come from, but for my money, you're a man to ride the river with!"

"Thank you," Slade acknowledged the highest compliment the range land can pay. "Now a strip of plaster for your lip. I'd advise you, see the doctor and have a couple of stitches put in. Otherwise you are liable to have a bad scar."

"Just make me even purtier than I am," Bartlett replied cheerfully.

Next, Slade turned his attention to the man Zack, the barkeep, had caressed with the bottle, who had been assisted to a chair and was gazing about dazedly and rubbing his bruised head. An examination convinced him that he had taken no serious harm.

The swinging doors banged open and Sheriff Crane stormed in, his other deputy and the two specials accompanying him. Also, Mary Merril, the cocked gun she held not exactly blending with her modish costume.

The sheriff let loose a bellow of wrath,

"So it's you, Bartlett! You and your Diamond F hellions! I might have knowed it!"

"We didn't mean no harm, Crane," Bartlett replied. "It was just a misunderstandin'."

"I'll misunderstand you!" promised the sheriff.

The very portly owner came wobbling from the back room at that moment, rubbing his eyes.

"What do you say, Cruikshanks," the sheriff asked, with a glance at an overturned

38

and three-legged table and the matchwood that had been a couple of chairs, "want to place charges against the hellions for messin' up your place?"

"Aw, to heck with 'em," replied Cruikshanks. "They woke me up with their blasted racket, but no matter. Drinks for everybody, on the house."

With this, all hard feelings were washed away.

"Say, what became of that iron you were packing in your hand a minute ago?" Slade asked Mary.

Miss Merril giggled. "An advantage to this long skirt," she explained. "I have a holster under it."

"Oh, yes, I remember now," he said.

"You do not!" was the indignant rejoinder. "I — never wore it before."

"That's right," he agreed soberly.

Mary favored him with a glare and refrained from further comment, changing the subject.

"Let you out of my sight for a minute and you're into something," she scolded. "When a man came running into the Branding Pen shouting there was a shooting over here, I knew exactly what to expect and came along with the sheriff."

"Glad you did," Slade replied. "Right

there with bells on, per usual. Where's Uncle John?"

"He was over at the Regan House, registering for rooms," she answered. "Wouldn't be surprised if he's along any minute. He'd have heard about it when he reached the Branding Pen. Yes, here he comes in now."

Webb puffed up to the bar. "Already raising hell and shovin' a chunk under a corner, eh?" he said to Slade. "I figured business would pick up."

Cruikshanks approached and was introduced to Slade, at whom he twinkled his little eyes set deep in rolls of fat.

"So you're the young feller who did for those two scalawags and got my dinero back," he said. "Glad you polished them off; they might have hurt Zack bad. Come in often. Everything in the house is yours from now on. Don't try to pay or I'll get hoppin' mad. Don't get me took that way. I sat on the last feller who did, and he ain't never been the same since."

"I can well believe he ain't, you ton of blubber," snorted the sheriff.

Cruikshanks winked at Slade and waddled to the back of the room to resume his interrupted snooze.

"He's all right," said Crane. "And don't let that fat fool you. He can jump three feet off the floor and kick a man in the teeth. He was a tough one back in the old days when he was a freighter. You have to be to get on the top in that business. He still ain't no snide when it comes to handling himself."

Something of the sort had passed through Slade's mind when he shook hands with the saloon-keeper and sensed the iron in the plump fingers.

Crane chuckled. "Ruckus sure didn't hurt business any," he remarked. "Joint is bustin' out at the seams; 'pears everybody's coming in to hear about what happened. A rowdy rumhole, all right, but no worse than a lot of others. All the ones close to the railroad yards are that way."

"I like it," Mary said. "Everybody seems to be having a good time. Reminds me of the Hour-glass over at Angelo, Walt."

"That's the mining town over close to New Mexico where they struck oil recently, ain't it?" observed Crane.

"Walt was largely responsible for the oil strike," Mary said.

"He's always responsible for something or other," grunted the sheriff. "Well, guess we'd better amble over to the Branding Pen and let Hardrock know just what happened; he'll be bothered."

"Anybody who takes up with this young hellion is due to spend a good part of his time being bothered," said Webb.

"And don't I understand that!" sighed Mary. "Not that there's really any reason to be bothered. He always comes out — never mind, Uncle Tom, I know what you're thinking."

The sheriff chuckled and didn't divulge his thoughts.

Bartlett and his hands, grinning and bobbing, wished everybody, Slade especially, good night.

"Hope to see you again," said the Diamond F owner. "Next time I promise to be good."

When they reached the Branding Pen, Hardrock was bothered, but not too much, having confidence in Slade's ability to take care of himself. Mary went on the dance floor with one of the Cross W hands. Webb joined some acquaintances at the bar, giving Slade and the sheriff an opportunity to discuss matters.

"And so you took Fletch Bartlett down a peg," Crane remarked. "He sets up to be plenty salty, too, and I reckon he is. I'll have to admit I been keeping an eye on him and his bunch of trouble makers. Ain't accusing him of anything off-color, 'cause I don't know, but I can't help wondering a mite."

"A newcomer here, isn't he?" Slade asked.

"Yep, been here only about four months," Crane replied. "Bought the old Quigley place over to the southeast and is putting it in first class shape; he's a good cattleman, all right, have to say that for him. That holding, you know, runs clear to the river, and it's a mighty lonely stretch along there; hardly ever anybody on the trail. Different from the one coming down from the north, which is pretty well travelled."

"Because of which," Slade said smilingly, "you are intimating that wide-looped stock say from John Webb's spread on the west and the other ranches to the east and north could be run across Bartlett's land to the river with very little chance of them being detected. Especially at night, and it would not be impossible to hole them up in the hills that are part of his range during the hours of daylight."

"No, I ain't exactly intimating it," Crane protested. "I'm just wondering a mite."

Slade refrained from arguing this somewhat casuistic differentiation. For several minutes he sat silent. Then he said:

"It is something to think on. Bartlett and his bunch struck me as being a hard lot with little respect for authority; throwing a punch

43

at the deputy sheriff wearing his badge is hardly in the category of a lawful act.

"Of course," he added, "turbulent young hellions when they lose their temper over something are liable to commit just such acts with little thought to possible consequences. But that doesn't necessarily mean that they are cow thieves or robbers. An excess of animal spirits plus the sort that dwells in a bottle can be responsible. As law enforcement officers, we have to consider all angles. But I repeat, it is something to think on. So far as I can see, right now we have nobody to suspect. Which means we must keep an eye on anybody who can qualify as a suspect."

The sheriff chuckled. "Darned if you don't make a better case against the hellion than I do," he said.

"Yes, but all pure theory on my part, just outlining what possibly could be but not necessarily is," Slade pointed out. "You can't take theory into court, nor does it justify Judge Colt justice, which is always questionable."

"Uh-huh, but effective," said Crane. "And I'm scairt it's the only kind that will work against the sidewinders operating in the section, like the pair we got bedded down in the office."

"Yes, there is an element of unpleasant truth there," Slade admitted. "Well, time will tell."

Mary returned from the dance floor and the discussion ceased, for the time being.

A little later, John Webb rolled over from the bar. "Goin' to bed," he announced. "Old bones need rest." He ambled out.

"Keep an eye on my young work dodgers, Walt," he said over his shoulder as he passed through the swinging doors.

The man who had been under discussion entered, his six Diamond F hands accompanying him. All grinned and waved greetings, but did not approach the table. Crane regarded them dubiously and glanced toward Hardrock to see if he had noticed their appearance.

However, the Diamond F bunch had only one drink and departed to the accompaniment of waving and grinning.

"Got to get back on the job, work to do," Bartlett called. "Goodnight, Mr. Slade. Goodnight, Sheriff."

"Hmmm! Leaving sorta early for a payday night," Crane commented thoughtfully.

"No law against it," Slade said.

"Guess that's so," the sheriff admitted, still thoughtful.

"Somehow, I like them," Mary remarked.

45

"They seem bursting with energy."

"No accounting for women's tastes, especially where men are concerned," grunted the elderly misogynist. "And they'll bust loose someplace, all right, you can lay to that," he added pessimistically.

Mary giggled, and did not argue.

Things were quite lively along the bar. Midway down the bar, a squat man with bleary eyes and a flushed face was mouthing something in a thick voice. Two men standing beside him, apparently having had enough of his yammering, turned and walked out.

The drunk subsided, mumbling over his glass. A few minutes later, he too weaved to the doors and lurched through them.

"Anyhow, things are sorta peace—" the sheriff began.

Bang!

Two more reports sounded nearby.

FIVE

"I knew it couldn't last!" roared Crane, leaping to his feet. He and Slade rushed to the door. Mary Merril whipped up the hem of her skirt and in a moment was right behind them, once again holding a cocked gun.

Outside was wild excitement, men swearing, shouting, gesturing to a dark alley mouth across the street. And on the board sidewalk lay the body of a man, face down.

"What the blankety-blank happened?" bawled Crane.

"Somebody cut him down from the alley over there," a voice replied, adding in injured tones, "damn slug — 'scuse me, lady — just missed *me!*"

Stooping, Slade turned the dead man over on his back. He was little surprised to recognize the drunk who had been sounding off at the bar, to the apparent disgust of the two individuals standing beside him.

"What in blazes do you make of it?" asked the sheriff.

"Only that I wish I'd heard what he was saying just before those two fellows walked out," Slade replied in low tones.

"You mean —" Crane began.

"I mean only just what I said," Slade interrupted, straightening up. He glanced at Mary.

"Talk about a quick-change artist!" he marvelled. "Where she took that smoke pole from nobody saw, and nobody saw when she leathered it again!"

"Women!" snorted the sheriff. "Just the same, she ain't bad to have along; three

47

irons better'n two. Show us how you did it, Mary!"

"I won't!" she answered, blushing. "I'll let you keep guessing."

The sheriff chuckled, but was instantly grave, and in very bad temper. He turned to the crowd, that was edging nearer.

"And nobody saw who downed him?"

There was a general shaking of heads. The man who had spoken before volunteered a bit of information.

"I happened to be looking across the street and saw the flash of the gun," he said. "Sorta lit up the dark for a second and I thought I saw two jiggers standing there. Didn't get enough of a look at them to say who they were, even if I'd happened to know them. Of course everybody dived to get in the clear of those blue whistlers, me, too; they talked mighty bad."

Slade nodded, feeling he had learned enough to confirm his own explanation of the shooting, which he kept to himself.

Deputy Estes hurried up. "Heard the shooting and hightailed," he said. "What happened?"

"Tell you later," Crane replied and turned to the crowd.

"Some of you loafers pack the carcass to my office," he directed. "Go along with 'em,

Bert." He turned to Slade.

"Guess we might as well go back and finish our snorts," he said. "Feel the need of one about now."

"First I want to have a look in that alley," Slade answered. "Hardrock," he said to Hogan, who, like most everybody in the saloon, was now outside, "fetch a lamp, please."

The lamp was quickly forthcoming. "Okay, let's go," said Crane. "And I'm going right along," Mary declared flatly.

"Okay," Slade agreed, feeling pretty sure there would be no excitement in the alley. He took the lamp and led the way, the crowd trailing along, at a respectful distance.

At the alley mouth, Slade bent over and held the lamp low, scanning the ground.

"Two sets of prints, rangeland boots," he announced.

"Is there anything you don't see!" grumbled the sheriff.

"They are quite plain," Slade said. "Let's see, now."

He led the way up the alley, slowly, again scanning the ground. After covering a short distance, he halted.

"Thought so," he said. "Two horses stood here. As soon as the devils finished the chore, they hightailed.

49

"All right," he added as the crowd pressed closer, "back to the Branding Pen. Nothing more we can do here."

At the table, Crane turned to him. "You figure then it was those two jiggers who went out just before the drunk that finished him off?"

"That's my opinion," Slade answered.

"Think you'd recognize them again if you saw them?"

"I would," Slade said. "Not that there's any evidence that they were responsible for the killing. Quite likely they will not show up here for a spell, but if and when they do, noting with whom they may associate could be important."

"But why did they kill that poor man?" Mary asked.

"Because he talked too much," Slade explained. "He was evidently sounding off about something they preferred not to be discussed in a public place. Alcohol in excess destroys inhibitions and loosens tongues. He may have been boasting of something in which he took part, or perhaps speaking of something he saw. Either explanation could be valid. So they proceeded to silence him."

Mary shuddered. "There are terrible people in the world," she said.

"But more good than bad," Slade replied gently.

"And sooner or later the good comes out on top," declared the sheriff, sampling his drink.

The killing was for a while a subject of discussion in the Branding Pen, with much wild conjecture and theorizing as to the why, by whom and wherefore. But not for long. Such incidents were too commonplace to the frontier country to occasion any very lasting impression. The drinks, the games, and the girls were of much more interest to the payday crowd. Soon the stark form with the two dead outlaws in the sheriff's office was forgotten.

Forgotten except by the two law enforcement officers to whom the drygulching posed a problem and a threat. Slade was fairly confident that the two killers, and possibly the slain man himself were members of the outlaw bunch terrorizing the section, and knew that if he saw them again he would recognize them. This could be important, possibly a clue to the identity of other members of the bunch and even its leader. Such an outfit almost always had a mastermind who did the planning and directed the forays.

There was one angle he did not want to

mention to his companions, for he admitted to himself that he could be wrong, although he did not think so. He had paid close attention to Fletcher Bartlett and his hands during their short stay in the saloon and he was almost certain, but not quite, that Bartlett had spoken to the two men who presumably were companions of the drunken babbler. It could mean little. But, on the other hand, it could mean a good deal.

"Suppose we amble over to the office for a closer look at that carcass?" the sheriff suggested. "Might have something on him that would be worthwhile."

"And maybe," he added hopefully, "Mary may find a reason for pulling her lead-pusher again and we'll see how she does it."

To this wishful thinking, Miss Merril's reaction was nothing more dignified than a disdainful sniff.

Upon reaching the office, they found Deputy Bert with the door shut and locked.

"Got tired of being pestered by the blasted squirrel fodder that were driving me loco with questions I couldn't answer," he explained, stripping a blanket from one of the bodies on the floor. "There he is, ornery looking specimen, don't you think?"

"About average," Slade replied. "And doesn't give the impression of being a hard drinker," he said thoughtfully. "Wouldn't be surprised if two or three snorts would set him off, which may explain why he had such a loose latigo on his jaw. Little doubt but he was spouting something he was not supposed to. A weak link in the chain, perhaps. Even a really smart outlaw leader can make a mistake when it comes to choosing followers. Could be the case here."

"And you figure there's a really smart hellion heading the bunch?" the sheriff asked curiously.

"Such has been my experience," Slade answered. "Almost always so, and the things you tell me have been happening hereabouts certainly tend to such an assumption."

"Which means real trouble," growled Crane. "That blasted Juan Covelo who operated here and finally got his comeuppance from you was a sample of what you're talking about, I reckon."

"He was," Slade agreed, "an outstanding example. I only hope we don't have such another to deal with, but you never can tell. And the very worst to cope with is the really shrewd and intelligent individual who somehow takes the wrong fork in the trail. Often they are the most ruthless, seemingly holding a grudge against all humanity, perhaps because of a real or fancied wrong over which they brood until it becomes an obsession and eventually develops into the blood lust. Altogether too many of that calibre."

Together, they methodically went through the dead man's pockets but discovered nothing of significance save quite a bit of money, a good deal more than a man dressed as a wandering cowhand would be expected to carry.

"Stick it in the safe till I figure what to do with it," said the sheriff.

"A good idea," Slade agreed. "For all we know to the contrary, the fellow may have been all right and somebody might come forward with information concerning him."

"From my way of looking at it, I figure he was all wrong, but as you say, never can tell," said Crane. "Well, reckon we might as well amble back to the Branding Pen and see how things are going. Maybe we can call it a night. Mary must be tired, packing all that heavy artillery on her."

"Don't worry about me," Miss Merril retorted. "I've packed — oh, shut up! The older you get the worse you get!"

The sheriff chuckled, and shut up.

They found the Branding Pen quite subdued. The girls had left the floor. The games had shut up shop. Only a few die-hard stragglers were at the bar. Crane ordered a last snort. Slade and Mary settled for final cups of coffee.

The bartenders were glancing suggestively at the clock. Mary also glanced at the clock, and at Slade. They said goodnight to the sheriff and headed for the Regan House through the almost deserted streets.

SIX

Shortly after noon, before he had breakfast, Slade carefully examined the ground in the alley diagonally across the street from the Branding Pen. With the greatest care he quartered the soft soil and arrived at a conclusion that he felt might be important. Leaning against the blank wall of a building, he rolled a cigarette and pondered what he had learned.

"No doubt about it," he told the brain tablet, "one of those killers walked with a decided limp, the boot heel prints definitely show it. Almost as if one leg were a trifle shorter than the other, or was injured. And I'm darned if I can recall if either of those two hombres who left the saloon shortly before the drunk was shot walked with a limp. Of course I could be mistaken; might have overlooked it. But I don't think so. I was interested in them because it looked like a ruckus starting at the bar, and followed them with my eyes as they walked to the door. If one was a hoppety-skip, I surely would have noticed it. This mess gets more complicated by the minute, with no definite answers to the questions involved. Well, I'll go eat; maybe that will help."

While he was eating, John Webb and Mary arrived, the girl bright-eyed and rosy. Slade glanced down at the hem of her long skirt and smiled. Mary blushed hotly and made a face at him.

After a while, old John pushed back his empty plate and announced,

"Got to be heading back to the spread. Don't like to be away too long, the way things have been going of late. But we'll be in tomorrow. Hope you'll be here."

"I hope so, too," Slade replied.

"If you're not, I'm liable to come looking for you," Mary warned.

"Artillery and all?" he asked smilingly.

"Yes, darn it," she replied. "You're having so much fun with it, I wouldn't deprive you, or the sheriff, of the pleasure. Take care of yourself, dear."

He promised and they left him to his coffee and cigarette, and his thoughts, which were far from satisfactory. For a while, it

56

had looked that he had a possible lead to the outlaw bunch in the persons of the two men who had preceded the drunken talker from the saloon. Now it appeared that lead had gone a-glimmering. Just possible, but highly unlikely, that they had signalled somebody holed up in the alley. That, however, was too vague for much consideration. Looked like he'd have to concentrate on some mysterious individual who walked with a limp, which was not very encouraging. Men who walked with a limp for some reason or other were not uncommon, especially right after payday. He pinched out his smoke and headed for the sheriff's office for a confab with Tom Crane, who, the waiter told him, had already breakfasted.

When Slade reached the office, he found Crane had a visitor, a slender, broad-shouldered man of above medium height. He had a straight-featured face with a firm mouth and light blue eyes — keen looking eyes. His dark hair was slightly sprinkled with gray. Slade estimated his age as somewhere in the late thirties.

"Hello, Walt," Crane greeted. "Want you to know Glen Graham; he owns the GG spread to the north of Fletch Bartlett's holding."

"Glad to know you, Mr. Slade," Graham

said as they shook hands. "Tom has been telling me a lot of good things about you. Perhaps you can lend me a hand: I need one."

"Yes?" Slade prompted.

"Glen came in with bad news, the only kind we've been getting of late," the sheriff interpolated. "He lost cows last night."

"For the third time in a month, between fifty and sixty head of prime beef stuff," Graham said.

"How was that?" Slade asked.

"I've been getting a shipping herd together," Graham explained. "Had the holding spot well guarded — three good men keeping an eye on the critters. But a couple of miles south of the spot is a big waterhole. Yesterday afternoon, quite a bunch was grazing around that hole. The boys planned to ride down today, round them up and add them to the herd. But when they got there, about mid morning, they were gone."

"Did your hands try to track them?" Slade asked.

Graham shrugged his shoulders. "What was the use?" he said. "They were evidently run off several hours before daylight, which gave them a head start, and besides, there's no tracking them over the heavy grass, which springs right up as soon as the sun hits it. Been a gray day or it might have been different."

Slade nodded. "And where do you figure they were run?"

Graham shrugged again. "There are a couple of fords south and east, where the river bows up this way, either of which can be negotiated by cows with the stream low as it is now," he replied obliquely.

"They'd have to cross Fletch Bartlett's land to reach the fords," Sheriff Crane observed.

Slade admitted it was so. But while he knew that Bartlett's holding was long from east to west, it was narrow from north-south, especially at that point, and could be crossed even by slow moving cattle in a few hours. He knew, also, just what the sheriff was hinting at, but refrained from commenting at the moment.

"So by now my cows are in the hands of Mexican buyers of wet critters and there's nothing to do about it," Graham summed up. "But perhaps you can help prevent a recurrence. I hope so, for I can't stand such a continuous drain on my resources."

Slade agreed. No rancher could.

"I'll be glad to do anything I am able to help," he promised.

"I'm sure you will," Graham said. "Well,

guess I'd better be getting back to see if the scoundrels have carted off the ranch house. Nothing safe that isn't nailed down, of late."

"And even if it is, some blankety-blank is liable to come along with a puller and draw the nails," the sheriff growled.

Graham laughed, and departed.

"A nice feller who's trying to get ahead," Crane observed. "He owns a slice of Tumulty's saloon over on Railroad Street close to the yards. It's a rumhole, but a money maker."

"I don't recall him from the last time I was here," Slade remarked.

"He wasn't here then," Crane replied. "Bought the holding about six months back. We've got quite a few new faces hereabouts. Bartlett, Graham, and a couple more over to the northwest. The old leaves falling one by one, you know. By the way, Pancho Arista, John Webb's partner in the carting business, was in and left just before you showed up. Said to tell you he'd be at the Branding Pen a little later, right after which he's heading for Marathon with a string of his carts following him. Seems a feller over at Marathon has a bunch of stuff he wants to sell and on which Pancho figures he can make a good profit. So he's heading for Marathon with a pocketful of dinero. Figures he can make it not long after dark."

"I hope he isn't spreading the information around," Slade said.

"You know Pancho keeps a tight latigo on his jaw," Crane reminded.

"That's so," Slade answered, his eyes thoughtful. "Well, I'll amble over to the Branding Pen and say hello to him; see you later."

When Slade entered the Branding Pen, he at once spotted a tall, broad-shouldered, strikingly handsome man with gray-streaked black hair, a firm but kindly mouth and piercing black eyes. Pancho Arista was Texas born, as was his father before him. But he was of pure Spanish blood. He and Slade were old *amigos* and the meeting was warm.

For a while they sat talking, recalling former adventures. Then Arista glanced at the clock.

"Will have to be moving," he said. "I suppose Crane told you I was riding to Marathon this afternoon to make a purchase?"

"Yes, he told me," Slade replied.

"A good deal of a ride, but Rojo — you remember my red sorrel — will make short work of it. The boys with the carts will be quite late getting in, but they don't mind. They get double time for night work of this sort. I'll be seeing you when I get back,

61

tomorrow or next day."

Slade watched him pass through the swinging doors, his eyes again thoughtful. He ordered coffee and sat smoking and keeping an eye on the clock. He let nearly an hour pass then left the Branding Pen and made his way to Shadow's stable.

"A little leg stretching in order, and possibly a little excitement," he told the big black, who seemed pleased at the prospect.

"Just sort of playing a hunch," Slade added. "But sometimes hunches pay off, and I've a feeling that this one will."

Arista had fully an hour's start. And Rojo, the red sorrel, was a speedy horse, but Shadow was even speedier. Besides, Slade knew a shortcut that would save many miles of riding. He was confident he could get ahead of Arista before the cart owner reached the sinister terrain farther west.

Soon he passed the lumbering carts. The carters, many of whom remembered him, shouted greetings. He replied with a wave of his hand and rode on, quickly leaving the cart train behind.

Now the mountains loomed closer. On the southern horizon were the peaks of the Bullis Gap Range. Directly ahead were the first of the ranges of the Trans-Pecos area. On the left were the far-flung ramparts of the

Big Bend wilderness. The mighty loom of the Santiago Range. The Haymond Mountains running obliquely southwestward, toward the higher peaks of the Pena Blanca Range and the still loftier ridges of Woods Hollow Mountains. Northward on the horizon was the jagged mass of the Glass Mountains. And on and on, invisible to the lone rider. The Chisos, high, many-colored, hazy, a serrated mass against the sky. Beyond, on the Mexican side of the Rio Grande, the Carmens, wonderful in their rich hues.

A wild and lonely land, this, with a fascination all its own. Luring the wanderer to adventure, romance and, ofttimes — death! Walt Slade rode on — one with the austere wastelands — understanding and loving every rock.

A few miles farther he turned off onto the little known, seldom travelled, forbidding, shortcut, running through a deep canyon that, unlike the winding main trail, bored straight west, abounding in pitfalls and rock slides, dared only by such an intrepid rider as El Halcon and a horse like Shadow.

The miles flowed back under the tall horse's speeding irons, his rider carefully noting certain landmarks. Abruptly he swerved north, a short distance beyond the canyon's west mouth, and quickly regained the main Marathon trail.

"Pretty sure we're ahead of him now," he observed. "We'd better be, the hunch is working. Yes, Pancho keeps a tight latigo on his jaw, as a rule, but perhaps not quite enough under certain circumstances. Also, not impossible that his various moves might have been correctly interpreted by watching eyes, of which there appear to be plenty in Sanderson. June along, horse, but take it easy. If something is going to be attempted, it should be somewhere along here."

Now El Halcon rode unusually alert, for he instinctively felt he was on dangerous ground. He scanned each bend in the trail before rounding it, hugging the growth that encroached on the track, where he and his black horse were almost invisible to anyone ahead. He paid particular attention to the actions of birds on the wing or in the thickets, especially bluejays and wrens, of which there were plenty. El Halcon could "understand" their language quite well.

It was not a noisy jay but a fluttery wren that warned him that all was not right. Well ahead, invisible to eyes less keen than El Halcon's, the little feathered songster was darting and swooping above a dense stand of chaparral that flanked the trail on the south, dropping almost to the tops of the brush, zooming up again, never settling to rest. A most unnatural action for that type of bird. Slade pulled Shadow to a halt at the edge of the turn that he had just rounded, eased him against the growth and sat studying the wren's activity.

"Something's got her bothered," he told the horse. "Something she doesn't understand and fears is close to her nest. Wrens will always react that way. Yes, I figure it's the same old thing we've encountered before, a nicely arranged drygulching from the brush, with a dead man left in the trail. One thing is sure, we're not ambling along that straight stretch of trail. Even though somebody is holed up there waiting, they might let us pass, realizing we were not their game. That would be a mite too much like gambling against a probably stacked deck. So into the brush with *you.* And stay put and keep quiet."

Shadow obeyed orders without too much argument. Slade dropped the split reins to the ground, bestowed a pat and stole forward through the growth. He moved silently but swiftly, for any minute now Arista might show. The faint, plaintive notes of the disturbed wren, caught by his remarkable ears, were all the guide he needed.

As he drew near the thicket where he figured the nest must be, he slowed his pace. Another moment and he heard the mutter of low voices. He slowed still more, almost to a snail crawl. He was now convinced that if the waiting killers who were holed up at the edge of the trail sighted him first, there was a very good chance that *two* dead men might well be their bag.

A couple more cautious strides and he saw the drygulchers, two of them, guns in hand, peering down the trail.

And at the same instant, Slade heard the drumming of fast hoofs, coming from the east. There was not a moment to spare! His voice rang out,

"Elevate! You're covered!"

SEVEN

With yelps of alarm, the pair whirled, guns blazing at the shadowy, shifting figure dimly seen in the growth. Both Slade's Colts boomed in unison. Back and forth gushed the lances of flame. The growth quivered to the vibrations of the reports.

One of the drygulchers crumpled up like a sack of old clothes. The other managed to fire one more shot before he, too, went down to writhe, stiffen, and lie motionless.

Flicking an oozing of blood from the back of one hand, Slade eased forward, guns ready for instant action, but there was neither sound nor movement from the two killers; he had gotten both dead center.

The beat of hoofs had ceased. Slade raised his voice again,

"All right, Pancho, I'm coming out. Don't throw lead at me."

There was an amazed exclamation, which loudened to an astonished shout as El Halcon stepped into view.

"Slade! What in blazes!"

"Take it easy," the Ranger replied, holstering his guns and starting to manufacture a cigarette. "Everything under control."

Sitting his red horse only a few paces distant, Pancho Arista stared as if he were seeing a ghost.

"What — what — what —" he stuttered. Slade's laugh interrupted.

"Just a nice little reception committee waiting in the brush for you," he said. "Don't worry, they're taken care of. Light off and have a look."

Mechanically, the still dazed carter obeyed; they entered the growth together. Arista shuddered as he gazed at the dead faces.

"They — they were waiting for me," he

stated rather than asked.

"They were," Slade agreed.

Arista was silent for a moment, then he said, in a strained voice, slightly mouthing his words,

"And were it not for you they would have — killed me."

"It is possible," Slade conceded. He thought it very likely, almost a certainty, in fact.

"I'm already so deeply in your debt it seems banal to thank you again," Arista said, continuing to gaze at the dead outlaws.

"They don't look to be so terribly bad," he commented.

"It is difficult to read character from facial expressions," Slade replied. "One can easily make a serious mistake."

Really there was nothing outstanding about the dead men, so far as appearances went. Just a pair of average range riders, the casual observer would say. Slade abruptly asked a question,

"Who knew you were packing a large sum of money with you, Pancho?"

"Why — why, I mentioned it to the sheriff," Arista replied. Slade nodded, and refrained from further questioning on that point.

"I drew it from the bank this morning,"

Arista added. "Of course somebody may have noticed me drawing it."

Slade nodded again, and again did not comment.

"I'll see if I can locate the horses this pair rode," he said. "Should be around somewhere close. Just a minute."

He stepped to the edge of the growth and whistled a loud clear note. There was a beat of hoofs on the trail and a moment later Shadow appeared, snorting inquiringly. Slade bestowed a pat on him and reentered the chaparral. Without difficulty he located the horses, tethered to branches. They proved to be docile beasts that offered no objection when he secured the bodies across the saddles, first examining the contents of their pockets, discovering nothing of significance save a surprisingly large sum of money, which he replaced.

"We'll pack them to Marathon with us and turn them over to Sheriff Chet Traynor, sheriff of Brewster County," he said. "He'll very likely be there, and it happened in his bailiwick."

As they got under way, Arista asked,

"How did you catch on to what those two devils had in mind?"

"I didn't exactly catch on," Slade replied. "I just played a hunch. This sort of thing is such an old story when an outlaw bunch is operating, and usually runs to a pattern; I've experienced it before. So I just assumed that such an attempt might well be in order and reacted accordingly."

"I see," Arista said. "But how in the world did you get ahead of me? I know you didn't leave Sanderson before I did, and you certainly did not pass me on the trail."

In answer, Slade explained his usage of the little known short-cut.

"But how did you guess the devils would be holed up where they were?" the carter persisted.

"That was from the birds," Slade smiled.

"Meaning?" Arista prompted.

Slade recounted the actions of the wren. Arista shook his head resignedly.

"Truly the Mexicans speak truth when they say that the eyes of El Halcon see all," he marvelled. "Well, as I said, I get deeper and deeper in your debt all the time. I suppose I was foolish to ride alone, carrying a large sum of money."

"I was surprised that you should do such a thing," Slade admitted. "Especially considering that you had a previous warning. You'll recall that a try was made for your cart train the former time I was here. That experience should have kept you on your toes, evincing as it did that the outlaws have an eye on your actions."

"Guess my brains are becoming addled in my old age," Arista said. "Well, I'll try and do better from now on; can't expect you to be always on hand to bail me out of the mess my mistakes get me in."

"Things didn't work out too bad," Slade said cheerfully. "The bunch is short a couple and Sheriff Traynor's treasury will be enriched — the sidewinders are packing quite a bit of dinero."

"Yes, as the saying goes, all is well that ends well," Arista admitted. "Just the same, it's not going to stop me from mentally castigating myself for being such a sublime idiot."

Slade smiled, and added a quotation of his own, " 'Honest confession is good for the soul.' "

He did not differ from Arista's expressed opinion of himself, reflecting that he spent a good portion of his time rescuing folks from the results of their own foolishness.

The burdened led horses slowed them, and it was long past dark when they reached Marathon, to find big, burly and jovial Sheriff Chet Traynor in his office. He greeted Arista, shook hands warmly with Slade.

"And what brings you here?" he asked.

"My horse," the Ranger replied smilingly.

"And trouble, too, on that I'll bet my last peso," Traynor declared.

"Just brought you a couple of presents prior to the holidays," Slade said. "Come out and take a look at them."

The sheriff did so, and swore with fervor.

"Might have knowed it, might have knowed it," he concluded. "All right, tell me how you came to collect 'em."

Slade did so, briefly. Arista added his own version of the affair, which lauded the part Slade played, with emphasis.

"Okay," Traynor said, "we'll pack 'em in and lay 'em out, then stable the nags. Imagine you fellers can stand a bite to eat — must be starved."

"A notion, all right," Slade agreed.

Now there were people in the street, exclaiming, questioning.

"Hellions tried to drygulch Slade and Arista," the sheriff said. "Tell you about it later. Right now we're hungry." He shut and locked the door.

The horses were placed in the stable the sheriff patronized, with the keeper Slade knew was dependable. He took time to give the tall black a rubdown and make sure all his wants were cared for. After which, they repaired to a big restaurant and saloon across the street from the sheriff's office, where they enjoyed an excellent meal. Arista hurried out to keep an appointment and spend the night with his friend who had goods to sell.

"You can get a room upstairs over this place if you hanker for a session of ear pounding," the sheriff told Slade. "You slept there once before."

"I plan to sleep a few hours, giving my horse a chance to rest, and then head back to Sanderson," Slade replied. "Something else may have cut loose during my absence."

"Always something cutting loose in that blasted hell town," growled Traynor. "Over here is plumb peaceful by comparison. An inquest? To heck with it! Arista will be here and he'll be enough to tell what happened. No sense in you riding back for it. I'll tell old Doc, the coroner, you ain't available."

Slade nodded. Such easygoing procedures were commonplace to the frontier country.

"A profitable day for the county," Traynor chuckled. "Those two horned toads were packing plenty, and the horses should bring a good price. What did you make of the brands?"

"Slick-ironed, mean nothing," Slade answered.

A little later he stretched out on a comfortable bed and slept soundly. Two hours before dawn, however, he was in the saddle and heading east at a good pace under the silver beauty of the stars.

Now the mountains to the south were a purple mystery flecked with patches of faintly glowing ash where the starlight reflected from naked spire and pinnacle. The trail stretched on before him, a pale ribbon shadowed by the encroaching growth.

The great silence of the wastelands was broken only by the weird cries of night birds and now and then the lonely, hauntingly beautiful plaint of a hunting wolf. Slade thoroughly enjoyed the ride and all doubts as to the future and the problems of the future were submerged in a sense of utter peace: while the stars lost their tints of gold, faded to pure silver, dwindled to needle points in the sable robe of night and vanished before the rose and scarlet glory of the dawn.

The morning was well along when he reached Sanderson, cared for his horse and made his way to the Branding Pen in search of some breakfast. There he found Sheriff Crane anxiously awaiting him.

"All right, out with it," Crane said. "I

knew darn well something was in the wind when you dropped out of sight like you did. What happened?"

Slade told him, then asked a question of his own,

"Tom, who was present when Arista told you what he had in mind?"

"Why, only Glen Graham," the sheriff replied. "Do you figure somebody watched Arista draw money at the bank?"

"Not beyond the realm of possibility," Slade conceded.

"Seems the loco coots will never learn," grumbled the sheriff. "I'd have had one of the boys ride with him if he'd asked."

"I'm very glad you didn't," Slade answered. "Especially if you hadn't mentioned his intentions to me; you might well have had a couple of cadavers on your hands. Personally, I wouldn't have cared to ride with him. Chances are he would have telegraphed our approach to that pair of killers, and I might not have been able to spot them in time."

"That I doubt, but could be," the sheriff admitted. "Didn't remember seeing that pair before?"

"Nor did Arista," Slade replied. "I thought of having Traynor pack them here to put on exhibition, but figured it would very likely be but a waste of time."

"Chances are you're right," agreed Crane. "Anyhow, they evidently weren't the two we figured killed that drunk who was sounding off in the Branding Pen."

Slade did not reply, but the concentration furrow was deep between his black brows, a sure sign El Halcon was doing some hard thinking.

Suddenly the sheriff chuckled. Slade glanced at him inquiringly.

"Some terrapin-brained galoots have been asking me questions about you," Crane explained. "Wanting to know if you are really El Halcon, and if you are, what am I going to do about it?"

"What did you tell them?" Slade smiled.

"I told them," the sheriff replied energetically, "to take a long running jump and see if they could make it to the middle of the Rio Grande in one hop."

Slade laughed out loud. "Fine!" he applauded. "That should hold them."

"Just the same, that blasted El Halcon business worries me," grumbled the sheriff. "I'm always scairt that some loco and mistaken marshal or deputy might throw down on you. To say nothing of a blankety-blank professional gun slinger who figures he could boost his stock by downing the notorious El Halcon, the fastest gunhand in the whole darn Southwest. And don't forget, he wouldn't be above plugging you in the back, if he got the chance. Not that there's too much chance of that — you 'pear to have eyes in the back of your head, but it does bother me."

Due to his habit of working alone and often not revealing his Ranger connections, Walt Slade had acquired a singular dual reputation. Those who knew the truth maintained vigorously that he was not only the most fearless but the ablest of the illustrious body of law enforcement officers. While others, who knew him only as El Halcon with killings to his credit, insisted that he was just a blasted owlhoot too smart to get caught, so far.

Others among this group were his ardent defenders, pointing out that he had never killed anybody other than some ornery sidewinders who had a killing long overdue, and that he worked on the side of the law and order with noted peace officers whose reputation was above reproach and who were not to be fooled by any owlhoot no matter how smart.

"You are right to an extent, Tom," Slade said. "But I feel that the advantages overbalance the risk. For instance, folks who would keep a tight latigo on their jaws in the presence of a known Ranger sometimes let something slip. And horned toads who figure me one of their sort just trying to horn in on their good things sometimes get a mite careless from wanting to eradicate me."

"Uh-huh, very much to their *dis*advantage," said the sheriff. "Oh, well, you always seem to make out."

And though he did not mention it, Slade thought of what was said by the Mexican *peones* and other humble folks, "El Halcon! the good, the just, the compassionate, the friend of the lowly!"

This, he felt, over-balanced all else.

"Guess old John and your gal will be showing up most any time, now," Crane remarked.

"Hope so," Slade replied; "they're good company."

"Uh-huh, but you'd better watch your step," the sheriff warned. "She hasn't yet evened up for the scare you gave over to the ranch house. She'll be out to git you."

Which Slade admitted was very likely and suffered a certain disquietude in consequence, wondering what turn her decidedly impish humor might take. He resolved not to be taken at a disadvantage, but was not overly optimistic. Miss Mary Merril was something to reckon with.

"Anyhow, I can get her flustered," chuckled Crane.

"Yes, but there's liable to be a day of reckoning for you," Slade predicted.

The sheriff looked uneasy.

Slade's prediction was due to be verified sooner than he expected. A few minutes later, he saw Mary slip through the swinging doors and, putting one rosy fingertip to her lips to enjoin silence, she glided toward the sheriff, whose back was to the door.

The next instant he leaped to his feet with a wild yell as a diamond-back rattlesnake draped around his neck.

EIGHT

The snake fell to the floor. Crane jerked his gun and fired two shots at it. The snake's head flew to pieces, but its body did not move. The room rocked with laughter. Only then, he realized it was not a live rattler, but a stuffed skin.

"What's the matter, Uncle Tom?" Mary asked sweetly. "You seem excited about something."

"You hell-cat!" he stormed. "You scared

me out of a year's growth!"

"Any growing you do from now on will be around your middle, so I really did you a favor," she retorted. "Sit down, I want a glass of wine. Uncle John will be here in a minute."

The flustered peace officer subsided to growls and mutters, and sat down. He glared accusingly at Slade.

"Did you put her up to that?" he demanded.

"I did not," El Halcon disclaimed heartily. "I just warned you."

"Uh-huh, and I warned *you*," Crane reminded. "You're next."

Slade feared he was right.

"And what have you been up to, dear, while I was away?" Mary asked.

The sheriff told her, and the laughter left her eyes.

"Always the same," she murmured. "Oh, well, perhaps I'll survive."

"I doubt if I will," the sheriff growled. "The whole room's laughing at me."

"Better to be laughed at than frowned at," she returned, cheerful again. "Where's my wine?"

Slade beckoned a waiter who hurried forward to remedy the lack. While she was sipping it, John Webb arrived and was regaled with an account of the frustrated drygulching.

"We're sure heavy in your debt," he said soberly to Slade. "It would have busted my heart wide open if something bad had happened to Pancho."

Mary Merril smiled tremulously as she recalled that the two men had been business rivals and mortal enemies until Walt Slade talked some sense into their stubborn old heads. To herself she repeated something she had said at the time of her first meeting with Slade,

"The understanding heart!"

Although it was still early, but a little past sunset, the Branding Pen was already fairly well crowded. Sanderson was, as a rule, a little quieter for a day or two after payday, but not much. Railroaders whose chores had forced them to remain on the job the nights before were now free to indulge in their own payday celebration. The same applied to cowhands who had remained on the spreads to guard against possible depredation. Plus town people who never passed up a chance for a little mild heck raising.

So there were still plenty of customers with money to spend, and they were spending it.

"Beginning to look like it might be another night," observed Sheriff Crane. "Getting so it seems every day is payday in this blasted pueblo. No rest for the wicked. None for the righteous, either. I feel it in my bones that something is going to happen."

Slade experienced the same disquieting premonition; something *was* going to happen before the night was over. What? He hadn't the slightest notion, which was the worst angle of it.

He studied the room. Everybody present, so far as he could ascertain, appeared innocuous and in a good temper. He muttered disgustedly under his breath and ordered more coffee. Hunches were all right and usually worked out but they were hard on the nerves, keeping one in a constant state of tremulous anticipation.

"Here comes Arista!" Webb suddenly exclaimed. "Looks like he got through okay."

"You sure made good time," he added as the carter accepted a chair and a drink.

"The boys were anxious to get back to town so they started rolling at daybreak and kept on rolling," Arista explained.

"No trouble on the way?"

"There was not, only wish there had been," Arista replied grimly. "That train was loaded for bear. Anybody who tried something against it would have figured he'd caught a grizzly by the tail. How's things here?"

"Just fine," Webb replied. "Except I understand Crane has started seeing snakes again."

Arista glanced inquiringly at the sheriff, who snorted disgustedly. Webb spared him for the moment.

"Satisfied with the bargain you made?" he asked the carter.

"Better than I expected," Arista replied. " 'Pears yesterday was my lucky day," — with a grateful glance at Slade.

"Uh-huh, you were darn lucky, lucky to have somebody to look after you," answered his partner.

"That you can say double," Arista agreed soberly. "Well, maybe I'll know better next time."

"I doubt it," said the still disgruntled sheriff. "Born terrapin-brained and you stay that way."

"What's the matter, Tom?" Arista asked. "Somebody put sarsaparilla in your glass?" He glanced down, spotted the stuffed snake skin, which nobody had taken the trouble to remove, and backed away hurriedly.

"What's that thing doing there?" he de-

83

manded.

"What thing?" asked Webb. "Say! Are you seeing 'em, too? Waiter, plain water for him from now on."

Mary felt an explanation was in order and proceeded to provide one, much to the amusement of Arista.

"So you see Uncle Tom was slightly *rattled,*" she concluded. "He has been having quite a bit of fun with me of late, but doesn't seem to appreciate the humor when he is the recipient."

Which persiflage Slade found entertaining, but it didn't do much toward solving the problem that confronted him; the problem of anticipating where the outlaws would strike next and, if possible, frustrating the attempt.

That they would strike, and soon, he was confident. They had missed out on two good hauls, which wouldn't set well with them, presenting the head of the outfit, with a problem, the problem of keeping his followers' pockets well lined. Which was highly important to such an individual, if one existed. Slade was convinced one did exist, and he had only the vaguest notion as to who the devil might be. Hardly a notion, in fact, just a hazy supposition with almost nothing to base it on. A chance remark, an otherwise apparently unexplainable incident. However, he had solved cases with even less to go on. Might work out this time.

A young cowhand of her acquaintance came over and asked Mary to dance. Sheriff Crane wandered to the bar to speak with somebody. Webb and Arista began talking business. Slade was left alone with his thoughts.

He began to grow restless, and a little tired of the continuous racket. Abruptly he stood up.

"See you a little later," he told the two carters. "Going to take a little walk." They nodded absently and continued their discussion. Slade waved to Mary, whose eyes followed him anxiously to the door, and sauntered out.

Outside, the air was cool and pleasant. There were plenty of people circulating, all animated and cheerful. Was going to be a busy night, all right.

For a while he wandered about aimlessly, studying faces, listening to scraps of conversation his keen ears caught. Abruptly he decided to visit Tumulty's place on Railroad Street, in which, according to Sheriff Crane, Glen Graham, the GG rancher, owned an interest. He turned his steps in that direction.

At this time of the night, Railroad Street, directly across from the yards, was rather dark and practically deserted. The tracks at this point were empty, but cars were rolling swiftly down the tall gravity hump to be shunted into designated track at the lower end of the yards, quite a few hundred feet distant.

Tumulty's saloon proved to be some way down the street, a bar of light that cut the gloom marking its site. Slade pushed through the swinging doors, over which came talk and laughter, and paused glancing around.

The place was not too large, fairly well lighted; the furnishings were not lavish but everything appeared clean. As he hesitated a moment before approaching the bar, a short and roly-poly figure advanced to meet him. He had a cherubic countenance with pursed lips and twinkling button eyes. Slade liked his looks. He thrust forth a plump paw.

"Howdy, Mr. Slade," he said in a piping voice. "Never saw you before, but it can't be anybody else. Tumulty's the name, George Tumulty. Glad you came in. Been hearing a lot of good things about you. My partner, Glen Graham, was talking about you this afternoon."

He chuckled and the button eyes, which Slade noted were shrewd, twinkled more than ever.

"Glen said some folks had told him they figured you to be an owlhoot. I said, 'That's right. Him and Parson Radcliff of the church around the corner often go owlhootin' together when the collection box ain't well filled.' He didn't think it was funny, but I did."

"I fear the parson would also look somewhat askance at your brand of humor," Slade replied smilingly as they shook hands.

"Oh, I don't know," Tumulty differed. "He's a jolly old jigger who likes a joke and is plumb fine in every way. Can be salty and tell everybody off if he's of a mind to. Sorta reminds me of a preacher I once met. He usta come into a saloon with a Bible in one hand and a six-shooter in the other and preach a sermon. Everybody listened. One night a galoot tried to interrupt. The parson laid his Bible down and belted him over the head with the barrel of the six-shooter. Then he finished the sermon, but the galoot didn't hear it. He was sound asleep on the sawdust. This ain't no yarn, Mr. Slade, it's gospel truth."

Slade nodded and didn't argue, for he knew the story was actually true, vouched for by unimpeachable sources; it really happened.

"Sit down, sit down," Tumulty invited hospitably. "We'll have a drink together, on the house."

"Be glad to, Mr. Tumulty, it will be a pleasure," Slade replied. Without seeming to, he watched two men who stood together midway down the bar. He recognized them as the pair who, a few nights ago, had left the Branding Pen shortly before the drunken gabbler was drygulched from the alley.

As they sat down, Tumulty assumed a more sober mien.

"Hear you've been doing some fine things since you coiled your twine here, Mr. Slade," he said. "Was mighty glad to hear it. Such hell raising as has been going on hereabouts of late is bad for business. My boys who come in are a rough-and-ready lot, most of 'em railroaders, but folks getting beat over the head and robbed and having knives stuck in their backs sorta upsets even them. Which I reckon is natural, seeing as they have to do a lot of their work in the dark and alone."

"Not unreasonable to think so," Slade agreed. "I met your partner, Mr. Graham, at the Sheriff's office the other day," he added casually.

"A nice feller," Tumulty said, beckoning a waiter to serve them. "I opened up here not long ago and have been doing all right, but I was sorta short on ready cash and when he said he'd like to buy a little chunk of the business, I took him up on it. He comes in quite often and talks with people. A good mixer, the kind you need in this business."

Slade did not argue the point.

As they sat talking, the two men left the bar and sauntered out. Slade was sure their eyes glinted in his direction. Tumulty, explaining an angle of the business, did not notice their departure.

A few minutes later, Slade finished his drink, thanked the owner and rose to go.

"Come again, Mr. Slade," Tumulty urged. "Always glad to see you."

"I will," the Ranger promised. "I like your place. Goodnight." He walked out and headed back up the dark street, glancing in every direction.

Almost immediately, his sharp eyes spotted two men sauntering along behind him, some seventy or eighty feet to the rear. Hmmm! Well, if they were looking for trouble they'd get it. He moseyed on. A few more strides and abruptly the situation became deadly serious. Coming from the other direction, at about the same distance as those behind, were two more men. If they had designs on him, and he believed they did, in another moment he would be caught in a deadly cross-fire.

His eyes swept his surroundings. On the right was an unbroken front of closed, dark warehouses. To the left, the unpleasantly open stretch of the vacant tracks, with no cover anywhere near. Things didn't look so good. The four men had quickened their pace.

Abruptly, he had an inspiration. A string of three cars was whizzing down the high gravity hump. On the front car stood a brakeman, brake club thrust between the spokes of the brake wheel, all set to slow the string before it smashed into the cars occupying the track at the lower end of the yard. Slade whirled and sped across the tracks.

He reached the racing string, reached up and gripped a grab iron of the front car which instantly swept him off his feet, dangling by one hand, swinging in between the cars, with the deadly wheels clicking under him.

From the street came angry shouts and a stutter of shots. Bullets hammered the side of the car. One ripped through the crown of his hat as he got a grip with both hands and whipped onto the end sill between the cars. Then he was past the killers, the string still racing.

Overhead sounded curses and a pad of running feet as the brakeman also sought cover. The speed of the string accelerated.

"Hold them!" Slade roared. "Hold them before they hit!"

More running above, more cursing. Chains jangled, the shoes ground against the wheels, too late!

NINE

Slade swung from between the cars, got a foot in the stirrup below the grab irons and peered ahead. The cars on the track seemed to rush toward him. He estimated the distance.

"Hang on!" he shouted to the brakeman. "They're going to hit!"

Letting go his hold on the grab iron and whisking his foot out of the stirrup, he struck the ground hard, rocking back on his heels. He lost his balance, turned a flip-flop and landed on hands and knees, shaken but unhurt.

With a terrific crash the string hit the cars. Overhead sounded a yelp of pain, and a torrent of profanity. If he could swear that hard, Slade concluded, the brakeman was not seriously hurt. A moment later he came clambering down, still expressing his opinion in language that smoked. He held up his lantern, the bail of which had been looped over his arm, and stared at Slade.

"Were those blankety-blanks throwin' lead at you?" he demanded.

"They certainly were not throwing kisses," El Halcon replied.

The brakeman rubbed his bruised head with his free hand, and glanced around apprehensively.

"Maybe they'll be coming this way," he said.

"I certainly hope so," Slade answered grimly. And he meant it. Now there was no danger of being caught in a cross-fire and he would welcome a showdown with the sidewinders.

However, the unsavory quartette did not put in an appearance. This did not surprise Slade. When they saw their try had failed, they very likely got in the clear as quickly as possible.

Now lanterns were bobbing in every direction, swiftly drawing nearer. The crash had been heard all over the yards and the railroaders were hurrying to learn what damage had been done. And Slade had to answer a lot of questions.

"Be seeing you," he told the bewildered brakeman, who stared after him dazedly. And he headed for the street. Walking swiftly, he rounded a corner and soon reached Main Street. Slowing his gait, he continued to the Branding Pen, after dusting off his knees with his bullet punctured hat.

"Say, didn't I hear guns shootin' somewhere?" the sheriff asked as he sat down.

"Not mine," Slade replied composedly, and with truth.

Crane regarded him suspiciously but refrained from further questioning, for the moment.

A little later, Webb and Arista left, declaring their intention of going to bed. Mary was on the floor again, so Slade gave Crane a brief account of his visit to Tumulty's place and his subsequent adventure.

"Those two hellions who were in here payday night are part of the bunch, sure as shootin'," Crane declared.

"Looks a little that way, but we have no proof they are," Slade answered.

"You didn't get a good look at the four who jumped you?"

"Fortunately they didn't get that close,"

the Ranger replied. "If they had, it might have been my last look."

The sheriff growled and muttered. "What did you think of Tumulty?" he asked.

"I rather liked him," Slade said. "Appeared to be all right."

"Strikes me as being a rather nice jigger," admitted Crane. "But the crowd he gets in that rumhole!"

"The majority of them didn't look too bad to me," Slade said. "Mostly young railroaders and young cowhands. A few I have my doubts about, but that applies to any place, even the Branding Pen."

"Varmints crawl everywhere," snorted the sheriff.

Mary returned from the dance floor, somewhat breathless, for the last number had been a fast one.

"You haven't danced with me once tonight," she said reproachfully to Slade. "I believe you get real pleasure out of seeing another man hug me."

"Vicarious stimulation, perhaps," he smiled. Mary sniffed.

Meanwhile a number of bar patrons had their heads together, casting frequent glances in Slade's direction. Finally, a delegation approached.

"Mr. Slade," said the spokesman, "I have,

94

but some of the boys haven't heard you sing. Won't you give us a tune?"

Mary and the sheriff added their voices to the request.

"Well, guess I haven't much choice," Slade agreed and made his way to the little raised platform that accommodated the orchestra, where the leader handed him a guitar. He made sure the instrument was tuned to his liking, played a soft prelude and sang.

There were those who said, with reason, that had Walt Slade chosen, he could easily have been a grand opera star. His great metallic, baritone-bass was pure gold and as it thundered through the room his entranced hearers would have heartily endorsed the declaration.

Slade knew his audience and sang simple songs that all would love. Songs of the range land, the hills, the valleys and the rivers, the rain mist on the amethyst grass heads tossing in the wind, the roar and clash of the storm, sunshine and peace, and the glitter of the stars in the silent night. Scenes of beauty, ofttimes of terror, familiar to the cowhands. Toil and sweat and blood, but laughter and reckless gaiety to leaven danger and tragedy and banish abiding grief.

Songs of steam and steel! Sagas of the men who guided the iron horse through sunshine and shadow, defying savage men and savage beasts to do their part in the winning of the West.

A hauntingly beautiful love song for the dance floor girls; and in conclusion, he sang of wide horizons, the wastelands, and the trail. A word picture that quickened nostalgic longings in the hearts of more than one of his listeners. Including, perhaps, his own.

So Mary Merril thought, for there was a wistful look in her beautiful eyes as he returned to the table amid a storm of applause, and her hand tightened over his.

El Halcon's musical efforts appeared to be in the nature of a climax for the night, because the crowd began to thin out. It wasn't long before the girls left the floor, the dealers shut up shop and the bartenders began glancing suggestively at the clock.

Mary Merril also glanced at the clock, then at Slade. Sheriff Crane chuckled, ordered a final snort as Hardrock sounded his last call. He accompanied Slade and Mary to the door, said goodnight and headed for his own domicile.

"Well, it hasn't been such a bad night," the girl said as they turned their steps to the Regan House. "Now suppose you tell me how you got that other bullet hole through your hat."

96

"Appears there's nothing you don't notice," he said. And he told her. Mary repeated a remark she had made before,

"Let you out of my sight a minute and you're mixed up in something. Oh, well, you always seem to manage to come through, and that's all that counts."

"If your number isn't up, nobody can put it up," he countered, doing a little repeating on his own account. Mary sighed and did not comment further.

A little past noon, Mary and old John headed for their spread.

"But we'll be back in a day or two," Webb assured Slade. "She'll be draggin' me in to put up with the smoke and the racket and the general heck raising."

Old John made his prediction in a mournful voice, but there was a gleam in his eye that belied it. In fact, Slade was pretty well convinced that Webb actually liked the bustle and excitement of Sanderson.

"Maybe you'll find time to amble out to the casa," Webb suggested. Mary seconded. Slade promised to do so if possible.

An hour or so later, Slade was in the saddle. However, he did not head for the Cross W ranch house but rode east on the trail at a fast pace, which he did not slacken until he reached a point from where he could see the river. Then he rode slowly, studying the stream and the terrain to the north. After a couple of miles, he left the trail and sent Shadow down the bank where there was a wide open space in the brush that for the most part clothed the bank. He paused at the water's edge, surveying the soft ground with eyes that missed nothing. At this point, a ripple extending to the Mexican shore marked a ford that, with this low river, could be negotiated by cattle.

"And cows have passed this way only a few days before," he told Shadow.

This was undoubtedly true and appeared to corroborate Glen Graham, the GG owner's claim that he had lost stock a couple of nights before.

For quite a while, El Halcon studied his surroundings which were far from satisfactory. The bank had been denuded of chaparral for nearly a hundred yards east and west of the ford. Save for on the one narrow track that led down to the ford, the heavy growth was replaced by jagged rocks, trailing vines, and foot-high thorn bushes with long and needle-sharp spines. It was practically impossible for a horse or cattle. A very bad terrain. Slade gazed at it and shook his head. Made to order for the wide-loopers.

Gradually, however, he evolved a plan that he believed might work.

Regaining the trail, he rode back to Sanderson, thinking deeply.

Reaching the railroad town with still a couple of hours of daylight to spare, he stabled his horse and sought out a general store where he purchased a hefty coil of fuse and a large container of oil.

"Nope, don't need any dynamite or caps," he replied to the dealer's question. "Just the fuse and the oil."

The dealer's curious gaze followed his tall form out the door.

"Now what in blazes does he want with all that fuse?" the dealer wondered to his clerk. "Bought enough to reach from here to the courthouse."

"Maybe he figures to blow up the courthouse," the clerk hazarded.

"Didn't buy any dynamite, and you can't blow up anything with just fuse. And why the oil?" The clerk didn't have an answer.

Outside, Slade remarked to himself, "Yes, I believe it will work, especially if the weather will cooperate." He glanced up at the sky, which was becoming overcast.

Reaching the sheriff's office, he outlined his plan to Crane, who shook his head resignedly, saying,

"If it was anybody else, I'd figure he was plumb loco, but you manage to come up with things nobody else would even think of, and make 'em work. Does look like it's going to be a prime night for a wide-looping. Betcha it'll be raining by dark."

"That's the way I see it, a perfect night for cow lifting," Slade replied. "And they are about due to strike. They've lost out on two good hauls and may be getting a mite short of cash. And the head of the bunch is likely to feel a little boost in morale is in order after losing four of his men within a few days. The others must be getting a trifle jumpy, a condition he can't afford."

"And if they don't pull something tonight, we'll try again tomorrow night, eh?" observed Crane.

"Exactly," Slade answered, "but my hunch says it will be tonight."

"You and your hunches!" snorted the sheriff. "Just the same, though, I'd hate to see you without 'em. You figure Bert Estes and Charley Blount will be enough?"

"I think so," Slade replied. "If things work out as they should, the advantage will be on our side and we know we can depend on Blount and Estes, which you can't always say about specials, no matter how trustworthy you figure them to be."

"That's right," agreed Crane. "Mean well but sometimes make some fool blunder that tangles the twine. Now what?"

"After you round up Blount and Estes and line them up, we might as well go eat. We'll meet here and not leave town until a couple of hours after dark."

He and the sheriff enjoyed a leisurely meal, then smoked and talked for a while. Blount and Estes were at the bar awaiting orders.

At the last minute, Slade changed his plans a little. As a result, Crane moseyed to the bar and told the two deputies to leave town alone, a little later, and await him and Slade at a designated point.

"May be a needless precaution, but with a bunch as shrewd as the one we're up against, it's best not to take chances," Slade explained. "Now I figure if anybody is keeping tabs on us, they'll very likely follow the deputies, and then we'll be behind *them*."

"And will they be surprised!" chuckled the sheriff.

After a bit, the deputies moseyed out. Slade and the sheriff waited a half hour and then also departed. They cinched up quickly and rose east on the trail.

Crane proved a fairly good weather prophet. It was raining from a heavily overcast sky, drizzling, rather, slow drop by slow drop, with a wind blowing from the north. Neither wind nor rain was heavy, but enough so to make the outside unpleasant, but ideal for gentlemen with cow-larceny in mind.

Slade carefully watched the back trail after leaving town, but saw no signs of a tail. A couple of miles farther on and the deputies rode from a clump of growth.

"Pretty sure nobody followed us," said Blount. Slade was convinced he was right. If somebody had, he and the sheriff would assuredly have spotted them.

"Okay," he said. "Speed up, we got work to do."

They rode on, chiefly by feel, for the night was pitch black, the visibility just about zero. But there were no obstructions or pitfalls in the trail, so Slade held a fast pace.

His uncanny instinct for distance and direction served him well, and he had no difficulty locating the track that led down to the ford. They descended without incident to the water's edge.

"Tether the horses well back in the chaparral over to the west, where they'll be out of danger from flying lead," Slade directed.

The chore was quickly accomplished and everybody got busy, breaking off twigs and branches from the growth and piling them at the foot of the bank close to the track leading to the ford, until they had a huge heap of the tinder-dry stuff.

"This ought to do it," Slade finally said as he secured one end of the fuse, which was wrapped with oil soaked cotton waste, deep in the pile. Then he proceeded to drench the fuse with the oil from the big container.

This taken care of, he carefully paid out the coil. He had made no mistake and the length of the fuse reached to the western stand of growth, and a little more. He dropped the end to the ground within hand's reach, beside his high-power Winchester. The others, at his suggestion, had also brought along their rifles.

"Better than six guns at this distance," he said. "Now all we can do is wait, and hope things work out right. Very likely we will be outnumbered, but circumstances and conditions being what they are, we should enjoy a certain advantage that should even the odds. We are law enforcement officers and must give them a chance to surrender, which they don't deserve. I'm pretty sure they won't, so if it comes to a showdown, shoot fast and shoot straight. Change position each time you squeeze trigger, so they won't be able to line sights with the flashes.

And if they charge us, which I doubt, don't give up so long as you have a cartridge left. Better to eat lead than to be pegged out over an anthill, or lashed on a cliff for the buzzards to pick your eyes out, either of which could be your fate if you fell into their hands."

The sheriff swore, under his breath, the deputies muttered uneasily. Slade chuckled.

"At least the rain has slackened to little more than a mist, which helps," he said. "And the sky is still heavily overcast, which is just as we want it to be. Sure you can smoke, only cup the matches against the chance of somebody watching across the river."

TEN

There followed a long and tedious wait. So long that Slade began to wonder if his hunch, after all, wasn't a straight one and that they had had a long and unpleasant ride for nothing. Sure began to look that way. But he took comfort from the fact that the hunch remained active. And after all, the wide-loopers, if they were on the job, would have made slow going of it in the black dark.

Then abruptly his spirits rose. On the

Mexican shore, straight across from the ford, a light winked, and again, and still again.

"That's the buyers over there signalling all is okay on their side of the river," he said. "Their elevation is higher than ours and the wind's blowing from the north. Quite probably they have caught the sound of the herd approaching. Keep quiet, now, and let me listen." A few minutes later he uttered an exultant exclamation,

"Right! They're coming. I can hear them."

His companions could hear nothing above the moan and mutter of the river chafing against its banks, but they took his word for it. A few moments later, they heard it too; the querulous bawl of a tired and disgusted steer.

Slade picked up the end of the fuse and stood listening, endeavoring to estimate just how fast the herd was travelling, just how much distance to be covered. He hesitated another minute or two, then said,

"This should do it." He struck a match, carefully shielding the tiny flame, and touched it to the end of the fuse.

There was a rain of sparks, then a little flower of fire travelling along the ground toward the oil drenched heap of dry stuff. With bated breath, Slade watched its progress, his ears attuned to the racket kicked up by the approaching cows. Still another moment and his strained eyes seemed to catch elusive, nebulous shadows flickering down the track. The herd had arrived! The wide-loopers would be bunched behind it and would doubtless allow the cows to drink and rest a little before putting them to the crossing.

Now he could no longer see the crawling flower of fire. Had the darn thing fouled up? His nerves tensed for action.

Suddenly there was a tiny flicker at the foot of the bank close to the track. Another flicker, a glow. Then a wall of flame that roared up, rendering the scene near the ford bright as day.

The last of the cattle had reached the water's edge. Behind them were seven horsemen who whirled in their saddles to stare at the fire raging at the foot of the bank. Slade's voice rolled in thunder through the night,

"Up! You're covered! In the name of the State of Texas!"

There was a bedlam of astonished and alarmed yells, a clutching of weapons, the blaze of a gun.

"Let them have it," Slade said and fired as fast as he could work the ejection lever. His companions' guns boomed an echo.

The outlaws fought back with desperate courage, but they were caught off-balance, utterly by surprise, and they could see nothing to shoot at save the shifting flashes of the posse's rifles.

A saddle was emptied, and another. Slade lined sights, squeezed the trigger, and a third man fell. Behind him sounded a curse; somebody was hit. He flung forward his Winchester, lined sights.

But at that moment, at a barked word of command, the four remaining wide-loopers whirled their horses and went charging up the slope, and his bullet missed. Before he could again bring the rifle to bear, they had reached the top of the bank and instantly disappeared in the darkness. Following them would have been sheer nonsense, for it would take time to secure the horses, giving the fugitives a long head start in the darkness.

The sheriff gave an exultant whoop,

"Fine! Fine! We did for three of the devils and got the cows. Not bad at all."

"No, not too bad," Slade agreed, his gaze fixed on the three bodies lying in the dust. "Only I very much fear the head of the bunch escaped. That was he, I'm pretty sure, who gave the order to hightail."

"Get a look at him?" Crane asked. Slade shook his head, but did not turn it.

"Hat brim pulled down low, neckerchief pulled up high, his face in the shadow. I was not able to recognize him as somebody I've seen, at least not definitely. Wasn't somebody nicked?"

"Little slice along my arm, nothing to bother about," replied the voice of Estes.

"Look at it shortly," Slade said, his eyes still on the bodies. "All right, stay where you are, all of you, and collect some brush to build up that fire."

Then he walked slowly forward, Winchester jutting to the front.

However, the heavy rifle bullets had done their work well and there was nothing to be feared from the three wide-loopers. He secured a burning resinous branch from the fire and held it aloft to show the brands on the cows.

"Thought so," he said as the sheriff advanced at his call, his arms full of brush. "John Webb's critters."

"And better'n a hundred head," replied Crane. "Like the last time you were here, you've saved him a big loss. The devils must have run them across Fletch Bartlett's holding." Slade did not comment.

"Hmmm!" commented the sheriff. "And

did you figure the one you took to be the head of the pack a big tall feller?"

"He struck me as being such," Slade replied, smilingly.

"And you didn't *definitely* recognize him as somebody you'd seen before?"

"That's what I said," Slade answered, still smiling.

"Oh, the devil!" snorted Crane. "There's no getting you to talk until you're of a mind to."

"A good deal of truth in that," Slade conceded.

"Then why am I wasting my time!" the sheriff grumbled. "Just the same, the trick you played on those hellions was just about the smartest ever."

"I had to figure some way to get the jump on them," Slade explained. "I certainly didn't hanker for a corpse and cartridge session with them in the dark. Sort of worked out. And by the way, the weather has sure played our game tonight. Look, the clouds are thinning, at just the right time."

They were. Another moment and they had shredded away leaving a clean washed sky glittering with stars. And in the east a half moon was riding.

"Will make rounding up the cows and getting them moving a lot easier," Slade commented. "Also, which is important, makes it impossible for those devils to turn the tables on us by coming back and pulling a sneak attack in the dark."

"You're darn right that's important," Crane agreed soberly. "There could be some more of them hanging around not far off."

He glanced to the north and slightly west as he spoke. Slade knew very well what he was thinking; Fletcher Bartlett's ranch house was in that direction. However, he refrained from comment. Instead he turned and whistled a loud, clear note. A few minutes and Shadow came trotting to him, snorting inquiringly.

"Now let's have a look at your arm," Slade told Estes.

The deputy's wound proved trifling. A pad and a bandage quickly took care of it. Slade glanced about. The cows, recovered from the fright imposed on them by the gun battle, had drunk their fill and were nibbling at the sparse grass at the foot of the bank, as were the horses ridden by the slain wide-loopers.

"We'll let the critters rest a little longer and then head them for home," Slade decided. "Now for a better look at what we bagged."

The three dead men were about average in appearance, no better nor worse than most cowhands or former cowhands. Neither Crane nor the deputies could recall seeing them before. "Maybe somebody in town will," remarked Crane as he busied himself emptying the pockets, discovering the trinkets usually packed by range riders, plus some money; not so much as from the pockets of the other four owlhoots, however.

"Guess the devils are getting a mite short of ready cash," he observed to Slade.

"Which means," the Ranger replied, "that very likely the rest of them will be making a try for something else without delay."

"Scairt you're right," Crane agreed. "About these cow critters, we're running them back onto Webb's pasture?"

"Yes," Slade decided. "And," he added soberly, "I only hope they were a bunch hanging around a water hole or a creek and not a guarded herd. Otherwise, we may very likely find a murder on our hands."

"I thought of that," said the sheriff. "Been bothering me a bit; I like all of Webb's hands."

Rounding up the cows and getting them under way was not much of a chore for experienced cattlemen and soon they had the thoroughly exasperated critters moving west on the trail. The bodies of the slain wide-loopers were secured to the saddles of the horses they had ridden in life, good looking animals with burns Slade quickly decided were slick-ironed and meant nothing.

"You'll be visiting Webb a mite sooner than you expected," chuckled Crane. "Well, he'll be glad to see you. Double glad, things being as they are. He's lost quite a few cows of late and he's getting tired of it.

"Betcha those buyers on the other side of the river were sorta put out," he added, with another chuckle. "Reckon they hightailed when the ruckus cut loose."

"Very likely," Slade agreed. "They don't hanker to get mixed up in trouble over here. Have enough of their own, dodging the *rurales*."

"And those Mexican Mounted Police are tough," said the sheriff. "They're the sort that shoot first and ask questions later. Well, let's see now. This bag tonight makes seven of the devils done for, the way I figure it. Wonder how many more of 'em there are."

"Hard to tell," Slade replied. "We know there are at least four, and it's unlikely that the whole bunch took part in the raid tonight. Well, we'll see."

The splendor of the dawn was flaunting its rainbowed beauty in the east as they drew near the Cross W ranch house. By the time they reached it, the sun was up, the bunk house already astir. They were greeted by shouts of astonishment and a barrage of questions. Slade let the sheriff do the talking.

His fears of a possible tragedy were relieved when he was told that nobody had been guarding a herd. Evidently the cows had been picked up around water holes or creeks. Three hands who patrolled the eastern edge of the spread had ridden in a short time before, reporting no activity.

"I can't understand how in blazes we missed spotting those devils, but we did," one said to Slade.

"It was a very dark night," was the Ranger's only comment.

Sheriff Crane, knowing there was more to it than that, shot him a suspicious glance, but held his peace.

"Next time don't curl up under a bush and go to sleep," the range boss suggested to the patrol. This obvious slander was received with disdainful silence.

Old John came storming out in dressing gown and slippers, to add his praise to the chorus.

"So you did it again, eh?" he said to Slade, after listening to a recount of what happened. "And if that wasn't the all-fired smartest trick I ever heard tell of! Guess those sidewinders figured the gates of hell had opened for them a mite sooner than they expected."

"Reckon they did open for the three we packed in," the sheriff said grimly.

Mary Merril appeared in a flowered robe, the color of which Slade thought went well with the deep blue of her eyes. She listened resignedly to what the sheriff had to say and didn't appear overly surprised.

"Come in, come in," said Webb. "Meat on the table. And then I reckon you'll want to go in for a little ear pounding. Don't worry about the critters. The boys will take care of them.

"Lay those carcasses out in the barn for the time being," he directed his hands.

A wrangler who had previously been introduced to Shadow took the big black to a stall, where Slade knew he would receive the best of care.

The Mexican cook had thrown together something special, in honor of El Halcon's presence, but enjoyed by all. Afterwards, they sought a few hours rest before continuing to Sanderson. Mary and Old John elected to accompany them.

"Maybe I'll be able to keep you out of trouble for one night," she told Slade, who didn't argue the point.

There was plenty of excitement when they reached the railroad town. People crowded into the sheriff's office to view the bodies. Nobody could recall seeing them before until George Tumulty, for whom Slade had sent, put in an appearance. He took one look, pursed his cupid mouth and nodded.

"Yep, all three of 'em were in my place a couple of times," he said. "Fact is, they were in yesterday afternoon. I think maybe Graham said a few words to them. He sorta makes it a habit to greet newcomers. Says it's good for business."

"Often is," Slade agreed. "Thank you, Mr. Tumulty."

When the crowd had thinned out and Crane had shut and locked the door, he observed,

"So they were in that rumhole, eh? And so were those two hellions who slid out of the Branding Pen right before that talkative poor devil of a drunk was drygulched from the alley. In there right before those four devils tried to gun-shoot you on the street and in the railroad yards. Sorta interesting, don't you think?"

"It is," Slade conceded. "But as I said before, there is no proof that the pair to whom you refer had anything to do with it."

"Maybe not," admitted the sheriff, "but just the same I can't help doing a mite of wondering. I hope those three under the blankets were three of the four. That would be plumb perfect. Well, guess your gal is waiting for you at the Branding Pen, so let's mosey over there for a snort or two. I'm feeling a mite dry."

They found Mary at the Branding Pen. She had changed her riding costume for something defying masculine description but, Slade thought, enhancing a charm really in no need of enhancement.

"Tonight you're going to dance with me or I'll know the reason why," she declared. "I'm tired of being a wall flower."

"Wall flower! With gentlemen on every side vying for attention?"

"That doesn't alter the situation in the least, and you know what I mean," she retorted.

"That's telling him!" chuckled Crane. "Don't let him put anything over on you, Mary."

"Well, if you are going to herd up on me, guess I might as well capitulate," Slade said, with a smile.

They danced several numbers together, then Slade relinquished her to another partner. Webb was at the bar, communing with some cronies, so Slade and the sheriff had a chance for a little quiet talk.

"Two things that puzzle me," Crane observed. "Why didn't Webb's patrols spot those wind spiders, and why didn't they plan to use the crossing a few miles farther east. It's much the better, and just a straight shoot across the south edge of Fletch Bartlett's holding and then right down, easy going, to the river."

"Because," Slade replied, "they moved the herd by way of Echo Canyon and the east-west trail."

The sheriff stared. "Huh! Do you mean it?"

"I do," Slade answered. "That is where the hunch really came in. I got to thinking, endeavoring to put myself in the rustlers' place and react as they would probably react. So I rode out there yesterday afternoon. Very quickly saw that cattle had used that crossing only a short time before. Very likely, the cows Webb lost not long ago were crossed at that point.

"All right. On such a night as last night, it would be highly improbable that anybody would be riding the Echo Canyon trail or

117

the east-west trail. And that route is much the shortest with the easiest going. Besides, the wide-loopers would know, shrewd as they are, that the patrols would be concentrating on the east edge of their holding and paying the trail no mind. So the cow thieves could count on little chance of being spotted. As you said, the crossing further east is much the best, but very likely the owner to the east of Fletcher Bartlett's spread would be keeping an eye on that crossing. Beginning to understand?"

"Oh, sure, now that you've put it before me," Crane grunted. "Old Captain Jim sure had the notion when he said you not only outshoot the owlhoots, you out-think 'em, too."

"It was all so simple and obvious," Slade deprecated the feat.

"Uh-huh, for El Halcon. What else?"

"You'll recall we agreed that, not having had much luck of late, the outlaws would quite probably be a mite short of ready cash. What would be the easiest and simplest way for them to recoup losses and replenish their exchequer? By way of a nice fat herd of wet cows. And as you yourself mentioned, last night, weather conditions being what they were, was ideal for a chore of wide-looping by men who undoubtedly know every foot of the ground and how to take advantage of the opportunities it presents."

"Then they didn't cross Bartlett's holding at all?"

"They did not."

"And that tangles the twine worse than ever, eh?"

Slade laughed. "So it would appear, on the surface, but not necessarily so. Admitting the hypothesis that Bartlett is responsible for the cow stealing and other depredations is correct, his position is unchanged."

The sheriff swore whole-heartedly. "Blast it! You get me more mixed up by the minute," he complained. "Do you figure Bartlett *is* responsible?"

"As I said before, I have no proof against Bartlett or anybody else," Slade reminded.

"Okay," growled Crane, "I'm going to ask you a straight question, do you have any notion as to who is responsible, who is the head of the pack?"

"Notion is the right word," Slade replied. "And only a very vague notion, based on nothing more than cumulative incidents that could mean a great deal, and then again, could mean nothing."

Mary returned from the dance floor at that moment and the discussion ceased.

"Now I feel better," she said. "I don't like

119

to have people thinking you neglect me. Oh, I know, I'm of secondary importance where your work is concerned, but I do like them to believe I mean something."

"If you don't behave yourself, I'll give them an example of how much you mean," he threatened.

Mary giggled, and looked receptive.

ELEVEN

The Branding Pen was well crowded. Webb and the deputies had spread around the story of the thwarting of the wide-loopers and Slade was again the recipient of praise and congratulations.

"How does it feel to be famous, darling?" Mary asked.

"Notorious would be the better word," he answered. "And I could do with a little less of it."

"You shrinking violet!" she scoffed. "You know very well you love it. And if you don't, I do. I'm very proud of you, my dear. Here comes Uncle John with several more prominent citizens. Get ready now to take a bow."

Finally things quieted down a bit and Slade was left in peace with his coffee and cigarette.

"Hello!" Crane suddenly exclaimed, "here comes Graham. He looks sorta tired."

Slade thought the GG owner did appear a trifle weary, his keen eyes red-rimmed as from lack of sleep. However, he was jovial enough as he approached the table, bowed to Mary and shook hands with Slade.

"Understand you're keeping up the good work, Mr. Slade," he said. "Everybody talking about it. And that trick you played on the cow thieves! Never heard the like. They sure must have been sold. Herd was run across Fletcher Barlett's holding, I suppose."

"The river can be reached by that route," Slade replied. Graham nodded.

"Yes, a straight run and an easy one," he agreed. "No, I haven't time to sit down. Having one drink at the bar and then heading for home; been a hard day. Wouldn't have come in at all except I wished to see my partner, George Tumulty, about a business matter. By the way, Mr. Slade, he is quite smitten with you; couldn't say enough."

"I'm glad he feels that way," Slade answered. "I like him."

"Don't come any better," Graham declared. "Well, be seeing you folks."

He approached the bar, downed a drink

quickly and with a wave of his hand departed.

"A plumb nice feller," said the sheriff. "Wish we could get more like him, instead of some of the specimens we do get. Wonder if Bartlett and his hellions will be showing up? Maybe they're tired, too."

"Darn it, I like them," Mary insisted. "As I said before, they always seem to be just bursting with energy and thoroughly enjoying themselves. Like a bunch of over-grown school boys."

"Uh-huh, they're over-grown, all right," snorted Crane. "Should have stopped growin' about thirty years ago."

"You're just jealous," Mary said, and made a face at him.

Slade sat silent during the passage, the concentration furrow deep between his black brows. A sign, both his companions knew, that "El Halcon" was in the ascendancy and doing some thinking.

Abruptly he stood up. "I'm going over to Tumulty's place for a little while," he announced.

"And not alone," the sheriff declared decisively.

"Okay," Slade agreed. "But you make me feel like a child in arms."

"Better to be a puling brat in arms than a

carcass in the dark," Crane said, rising, and hitching his cartridge belt a little higher. "Don't you think so, Mary?"

"I sure do," she replied as she also stood up.

"You, too!" the Ranger exclaimed.

"Uh-huh, me too," she answered. "I want to see that rowdy place you've both been talking about; I like rowdy places."

"Got your artillery with you?" he asked.

"I sure have," she said. "All set to use it, too. Only I hope I won't have to climb up the side of a boxcar in this skirt." *

"Not likely you'll need to," he returned. "I hardly look for a repeat performance so soon. All right, let's go.

"Be back shortly," he called to Webb, who was still at the bar. "And I'm going to bed shortly," old John called back. "See you tomorrow."

"He's very considerate," said Mary with another giggle. "Say, this night air feels good after all the smoke and smells. I hope your rumhole, as Uncle Tom calls it, is draftier."

"It is," Slade told her. "Usually most of the windows knocked out."

"Sounds very interesting," she replied.

The sheriff was very much on the alert as they walked dark Railroad Street. Slade, however, gave but cursory attention to his surroundings, being confident that nothing untoward would happen.

"Well, here we are," he said as they reached the saloon without incident.

Tumulty hurried to greet them, his rubicund countenance wreathed in smiles. He insisted in doing the serving himself.

"I'm honored, plumb honored," he declared, bowing to Mary, though his body was not formed to bend that way. "Mind if I join you?"

"We were hoping you would," the girl told him. Slade and the sheriff seconded the invitation. Tumulty sat down, diffidently.

Slade searched the room with his eyes, in quest of certain faces. But the two men whose comings and goings had interested him were conspicuous for their absence.

The patrons were much the same as on the occasion of his previous visit, railroaders, cowhands, and others. A noisy and somewhat rowdy crowd, but for the most part harmless enough, he concluded.

Mary also looked around. "I like this place," she said. "Nice girls you have on the floor, Mr. Tumulty. Wonder if I could get a job here."

The suggestion evidently delighted and amused the owner, for he chuckled wholeheartedly.

"What do you say, Mr. Slade?" he asked.

"I say you have troubles enough without looking for more," the Ranger replied. "She'd have the whole place by the ears in no time flat; she has a positive genius for it."

"Think I'd be willing to take a chance," Tumulty said with another chuckle.

"Your partner, Mr. Graham, dropped in at the Branding Pen for a few minutes," Slade remarked casually. "Said he was tired and was going home."

"He was here earlier in the evening," Tumulty answered. "He did look tired. He's short-handed and the ranch keeps him busy. He has his troubles. Has been losing stock and can't afford it. Keeps him scratching to meet the payments on his holding. I advanced him a bit of money from the business. He was very grateful. I was glad to be able to do it; he's a nice feller."

"Gives that impression," Slade conceded, his eyes thoughtful, and Mary, familiar with all his moods, instantly noted. Her own delicate brows drew together a trifle.

"About those three cow thieves you have laid out in the office," Tumulty suddenly remarked, "I mentioned 'em to Graham and he sorta remembered speaking with them when they were here. Said he gathered they

125

were chuck line riders from Arizona. Wouldn't be surprised if Arizona got too hot for them and they moved over here, where they found it even hotter. Guess they're cool enough, now."

"Depends on what the hereafter is," suggested the sheriff. "If it's what we're taught to believe, I've a notion they're plenty hot about now, and busy playin' their coal shovels. What do you think, Walt?"

"You may have the right of it," Slade conceded. "Incidentally, I believe, only I'm not quite sure, that the burns on their horses are slick-ironed Arizona brands, which will tend to substantiate their claim. That is of moving here from Arizona. Interesting."

Crane glanced at him inquiringly, but Slade did not pursue the subject. Instead, he glanced at the clock and suggested,

"Really, I think we should be going, it's quite late."

"Come again," Tumulty urged. "Always be plumb glad to see you. And Miss Merril, that job on the dance floor is wide open any time you can get Mr. Slade to agree."

"He's an old grouch," Mary replied. "I think he's afraid to take a chance on me."

"Hmmm!" remarked the sheriff. "I've a notion he's already took that sort of a

126

chance."

"*Will* you tighten the latigo on your jaw!" Mary requested. "Heavens above! I'm beginning to talk like a cowhand!"

"Well, you don't look like one," Crane said. "Let's go!"

TWELVE

Mary and old John returned to the spread shortly after noon. Slade promised to pay them a visit soon. An hour later an inquest was held on the collection of bodies in the sheriff's office, which, to nobody's surprise, exonerated the posse members from all blame in killing the outlaws and commended them for doing a good chore.

"Floor's all nice and empty now," observed the sheriff to Slade, after coroner and jury had departed in search of needed refreshment. "Yep, all empty, but not for long, I hope. What you thinking?"

"I'm thinking," Slade replied, "that we can look for trouble very soon. "I'm convinced the bunch is running short of money, after losing three good hauls, one after another in but a few days. Yes, they're feeling the pinch and will strike somewhere soon. And this time I haven't the slightest notion where."

"Just go ahead and dig up another hunch," the sheriff advised cheerfully.

"Easier said than done," Slade smiled.

"You'll do it," declared Crane, still cheerful. "No doubt in my mind as to that."

"Hope you're right," Slade said, "for I sure need one right now."

"Maybe a snort and a snack will help," said the sheriff. "Let's try it."

They did, but after a sandwich and several cups of coffee, El Halcon was still short of inspiration.

For some time, they sat in silence, the sheriff puffing furiously on his pipe. Slade gazed out the window at the sun dappled street, the ever changing groups of people. Those groups had a never ceasing interest for El Halcon. Abruptly he stood up.

"Going for a walk," he announced.

"Okay," replied Crane. "Keep your eyes open." Slade promised, carelessly, to do so, and departed.

For quite some time, he wandered along Main Street, scanning faces, listening to conversations. He stood on a corner and gazed absently at the gold and purple magic of the mountains, though really hardly seeing them, for his thoughts were elsewhere.

He could always think better in the open air, and he felt he had plenty to think about.

He was convinced that the outlaws would strike again and soon. His earnest hope was to be able to anticipate where the attempt would be made, which would afford a chance to thwart it.

There were so blasted many things they could hit! Stage coaches, banks, big stores, trains. He did not believe there would be any more wide-looping for a while. Their number was undoubtedly depleted and it required considerable man power to successfully rustle a big herd.

Finally he turned his steps to Railroad Street and strolled along, what was at this time of day, a busy thoroughfare. To his right was the bustling activity of the railroad yards. Cars whizzed down the gravity hump and onto a newly built lead to the tracks of the lower yard.

Suddenly there was a terrific crash and a banging and thudding. He glanced in the direction of the sound and quickened his gait.

Three loaded box cars lay on their sides, their wheels spinning futilely. Two tracks were blocked, but the lead was clear. A bruised and battered brakeman was rising from the ground, swearing wholeheartedly, evidently not badly hurt by his tumble from the top of an overturned car. Shouting railroaders were running from all directions to the scene of the wreck.

Reaching the lead, Slade walked along it, studying the tracks. He glanced at the gravity hump, glanced back at the rails, and shook his head.

"Twice in two days!" bawled an angry yard conductor. "What the blankety-blank-blank is wrong, anyhow?"

Slade could have told him, but did not. He continued to study the lead.

"Here comes the super!" exclaimed the conductor.

The yards and shops superintendent, a dignified looking elderly man, hurried forward. Abruptly he paused, gazing at El Halcon, and extended his hand.

"Mr. Slade, isn't it?" he said. "Never met you before but heard you described. My name's Sutton, Peleg Sutton," he added as they shook hands. "Heard a lot about you, especially from Mr. O'Brien, the general division superintendent. He was telling me how you rectified a defect in the gravity hump when you were here formerly. This wasn't my station then. Mr. O'Brien holds you in high esteem. What do you think of this mess?"

"I think," Slade said quietly, "that somebody erred."

"Yes?"

"Yes. That lead was not properly run. The double curve is a trifle too sharp, and the elevation of the outer rails is not sufficient. Instead of clamping the flanges against the inner rail, it tends to raise them. Raise them a bit too much and they climb the rail, and over she goes. A single car will usually get through, but not a string, as in the present instance, when you have drawbar pull to contend with."

Sutton bristled a little. "Mr. Slade," he said, "I think you are mistaken. I laid out that lead myself and I am sure there is nothing wrong with it."

"Have you a transit and a measuring rod, and somebody I can instruct how to handle the rod?" Slade asked. "And a measuring chain and stakes? If so, fetch them."

"I can handle the rod, if you can handle the transit," Sutton replied doubtfully. He dispatched a man on the errand who returned shortly with the necessary tools.

Slade took the transit and examined it. "The one I used before," he said. "A good instrument, equipped with spirit level on the telescope, and magnetic compasses. The universal tool of the surveyor."

Sutton blinked, but held his peace while Slade instructed him just where to hold the

131

rod with its graduated numbers. Two men were chosen to handle the chain and the stakes.

Setting the transit, making sure the tripod was firmly based, Slade took a sight, called the result to Sutton, who confirmed it. He took another sight, showed the men with the chain where to drive their stakes, drew a notebook and pencil from his pocket and jotted down the results. Re-setting the transit and the rod, he repeated the maneuver. A third sight, and still another. Moving the transit well back, he focused the telescope on the rod once more.

"That should do it," he said and went to work on the notebook. Figures and symbols flowed under his slim fingers. An equation took form, and its solution. He tore out the sheet, handed it to Sutton.

"There is the double curve, and the proper rail elevation," he said. "Look them over."

As the super did so, his brows knit. He stared at the figures, went over them again, muttering to himself. Finally he swore a disgusted oath.

"Mr. Slade," he said, "I was wrong and you are right. How in blazes did I come to make such a stupid mistake!"

"Doesn't everybody make them?" Slade

consoled him, smiling for the first time.

"Yes, there's the line for your steel," he added. "All you need to do is get your crew busy on it. You won't have any more trouble."

"You're darn right," agreed Sutton. "You are an engineer, Mr. Slade," he stated, rather than asked.

"I know something of the principles of engineering," Slade replied.

"Huh!" snorted Sutton. "I'd say you are the gent who invented 'em."

Aside from, under the circumstances, pardonable exaggeration, Sutton wasn't too far off, as such men as General Division Superintendent O'Brien, James G. "Jaggers" Dunn, the famous General Manager of the great C. & P. Railroad System, former Texas Governor Jim Hogg, and John Warne "Bet-a-Million" Gates would testify.

Shortly before the death of his father, which occurred after financial reverses that occasioned the loss of the elder Slade's ranch, young Walt had graduated from a noted college of engineering. He had planned to take a post graduate course in certain subjects to round out his education and better fit him for the profession he hoped to make his life work. Since that was economically impossible at the time, he lent a receptive ear when Captain Jim McNelty, the famed Commander of the Border Battalion of the Texas Rangers, suggested he come into the Rangers for a while and pursue his studies in spare time.

"You seemed to like the work when you were with me during summer vacations," Captain Jim had said. "Maybe you'll get to like it better."

That was the catch. Slade did learn to like Ranger work, more and more. Long since he had gotten more from private study than he could have hoped for from schooling and was eminently fitted for the profession of engineering.

But Ranger work provided so many opportunities to help the deserving, to right wrongs, and serve his fellowmen. He was loath to sever connections with the illustrious body of law enforcement officers. An engineer? Yes, eventually, but not just yet.

More than once and more than twice his engineering knowledge had, directly or indirectly, furthered his Ranger work. And the incident just completed would do just that.

"Seems you're always pulling this blasted railroad out from under somebody's foolish mistake," Sutton continued. He added, jokingly,

"Maybe you'd better make it a point to see the westbound Flyer doesn't turn over tonight. If she does, there'll be a lot of disappointed people hereabouts."

"How's that?" Slade asked.

"The new big machine shop and the extension of the yard were completed today," Sutton explained. "The contractors and their workers expect to get paid tomorrow, and the Flyer is packing in the money in the express car safe. It will be put in the bank; quite a sum."

"I see," Slade said, his eyes abruptly very thoughtful. "And the Flyer will be due in Sanderson shortly after dark."

"That's right," replied Sutton. "Oh, she'll make it all right: excellent roadbed from here east. Haven't had any trouble on it for a long time; O'Brien keeps his division in first-class shape. And —" twinkling his eyes at Slade — "he doesn't allow me to monkey with the curves."

"I think he'd be safe in taking a chance," Slade replied.

A track gang was already busy at work on the lead. Slade watched them for a few minutes, decided they knew their business and that he would no longer be needed.

"So I'll be seeing you, Mr. Sutton," he said. "Have to be getting back to the sheriff's office."

"I certainly hope so," answered Sutton. "Where do you hang out of evenings?"

"Mostly in the Branding Pen," Slade replied.

"Okay, I'll be seeing you there," Sutton promised. "And thank you for everything."

Slade sauntered from the yard. But when he reached the street, he quickened his pace. Very shortly, he regaled Sheriff Crane with an account of the happenings in the yard, including Sutton's chance remark about the Flyer bringing in the money to pay the contractors and their large force of workers.

"So this time we'll be working on something more concrete than just a hunch," he concluded. "The reward, perhaps, for lending a helping hand."

"You figure the devils will make a try for that money?" Crane asked.

"One thing is sure for certain, they're being handed a grand opportunity," Slade replied. "It appears to be common knowledge that the Flyer is packing the money, and I figure the head of the bunch is in a position to learn things. If they do attempt something, I'm pretty sure I know where it will be. There's just one really good spot between here and Langtry, and it happens to be made to order for them. Just above twelve miles to the east of here; we'll have time to make it before the Flyer shows, if we hustle a little. Round up your deputies and let's go. We have nothing to lose and perhaps a lot to gain, plus perhaps saving somebody from getting murdered. It's a killer bunch. Okay, I'll tie onto my cayuse and meet you here."

The sheriff hurried out to locate Blount and Estes, while Slade repaired to Shadow's stable.

Crane had the luck to find the deputies where he had hoped to find them, in the Branding Pen putting away a snack. So all three arrived at the stable while Slade was cinching up. A few minutes later, the posse rode east at a fast pace.

For a while, Slade scanned the back trail, although he thought there was little chance that they would be followed. If the outlaws did contemplate a raid on the passenger train, it was logical to believe that the whole bunch would be on the job. And at any rate, nobody could pass the posse without being spotted. Which was all that really mattered.

The miles flowed back under the horses' speeding irons. Slade glanced at the westering sun, estimated the distance they had to cover and the time the Flyer should be expected to reach the designated spot. He decided they had plenty of time to reach the vicinity and make the necessary maneuvers. And as he rode, by the minute, the feeling that the outlaws would really make a try for the money the Flyer packed grew stronger.

"Hope it's working up to a hunch," the sheriff chuckled. "I got faith in your hunches; they always seem to work out."

Just the same, the sheriff knew that what El Halcon called a hunch was really the result of painstaking thinking and a meticulous analyzing of circumstances and conditions. When Walt Slade believed a thing was going to work out a certain way, it almost always did just that.

With the sun low in the west, they finally reached the bottom of a long and gentle slope that stretched up and up for hundreds of yards. Where it dipped over the summit, the trail stood out hard and clear against the sky, but on either side, brush encroached on the track.

"From now on, we take it easy," Slade said. "Down at the bottom of the far sag is where they'll pull it, if they're going to. The spot is ideal. Plenty of brush to provide cover, a rather sharp curve that gives the engine crew vision of but a short distance.

But the train will be coming around it rather fast to make the run for the grade up the sag, which is quite stiff. An obstruction on the track and the train will either hit it or have to stop.

"And now comes the ticklish part," he added. "I don't think they'll have somebody up there keeping a watch on the trail this way, but if they have, well — it's been nice knowing all of you."

"Oh, shut up!" growled the sheriff. "I've got the shakes already without you making 'em worse."

Slade chuckled, and slowed the pace.

It was a nerve-wracking business, pacing slowly up the slope toward that ominous crest, not knowing from one minute to the next but that it would erupt a roaring blast of gunfire. A horse coughed. The sheriff and deputies jumped in their hulls, then swore under Slade's amused glance.

"We have to get nearly two-thirds of the way up the slope before the brush is thin enough to turn into it," he said. "Take it easy."

Slade's eyes never left the crest that drew steadily nearer. He watched the tops of the chaparral for any swaying that might indicate somebody moving under it, noted carefully the movements of the few birds flitting about, his ears attuned to any alien sound.

Up and up, with the tension heightening. Maybe the hidden outlaw in the growth was just waiting until a miss would be impossible. Slade's vivid imagination could vision the forward thrusting rifle barrel, the evil eyes glancing along the sights, the finger tightening and tightening on the trigger. He knew very well he would be the prime target. At any moment the gush of flame he would see; the boom of the report he would not hear; a rifle bullet travelling faster than sound. He tightened his jaw and led the way.

Finally, they were more than two-thirds up the sag and he said, instinctively holding his voice down,

"Looks like we made it; now into the brush."

There was a general sigh of relief as they eased the horses into the thinner straggle, through which they could pass without undue noise. Now the odds were a bit more even. Very shortly they reached the crest and slipped forward to a final fringe of leaves and twigs.

Every now and then, while mounting the slope, they had caught glimpses of the railroad, which here edged toward the trail but several hundred feet lower down. Now it lay before them. Directly below, the rails were in the shadow, but at the beginning of the sharp curve to the east, they gleamed in the reddish sunlight. It was a good five hundred yards to where the curve began. There Slade was confident the attempt would be made, were one in the making. But it certainly didn't look like it.

"Would appear we have been riding a cold trail," he remarked. "No obstruction on the track, nobody hanging around with a red flag. Well, here comes the Flyer, I can hear the exhaust. We might as well stick around until she passes."

Louder and louder sounded the chatter of the locomotive exhaust. Now Slade could hear the rumble of the wheels. He relaxed in the saddle and waited.

Around the curve boomed the Flyer, exhaust crackling, side rods flashing a blur.

"Well," began the sheriff. "God A'Mighty!"

THIRTEEN

The exhaust had snapped off. There was a screech of brake shoes grinding the wheels. But the train rushed on.

Suddenly the speeding locomotive lurched and swayed wildly. Over it went on its side, with a terrific crash, steam howling from

141

broken pipes. The baggage car slewed around, turned over and went sliding down the embankment. The express car left the rails and hung swaying and teetering. The coaches behind bucked and jumped.

"The devils removed a rail!" Slade shouted. "The engineer didn't see it in time."

Out of the heavy growth fringing the track bulged seven men, shooting at the coaches, the express car and the engine cab.

"After them!" Slade roared. "Ride and shoot!"

Down the slope through the straggle of low growth tore the posse. Slade flung his Winchester forward, fired as fast as he could squeeze trigger, the ejection lever a flashing blur. If a shell jammed, it would snap like matchwood.

The outlaws whirled at the sound. Fire spurted, bullets whined past. The posse blazed a volley.

An outlaw fell forward on his face. Another slumped sideways to the ground to lie motionless. Slade slammed his empty rifle into the boot and shipped out his Colts, shooting with both hands.

A third raider reeled around and around, a bullet through his middle. He went down, writhed, jerked and stiffened out.

A voice bellowed a command. The four remaining owlhoots dashed frantically into the chaparral. There sounded a prodigious crashing as they mounted their horses and fled east. To follow them was impractical. Slade's interest focused on the overturned locomotive, the wooden cab of which was burning fiercely, and the engine crew.

"I slipped," he said bitterly, "I should have known the cunning devil had something real smart up his sleeve."

"Don't see what you could have done about it," jolted the sheriff. "And we didn't do too bad."

They reached the right-of-way. With a glance at the bodies, Slade holstered his guns and flung himself from the saddle.

The fireman, bruised and bloody, was running around in circles, pointing to the burning cab.

"He's in there! He's in there!" he yammered. "Old Tom's in there! He'll be burned up!"

Slade rushed to the cab, barely managed to squeeze through the slanting gangway. The cab was filled with smoke, hot steam and flame. Peering with strained eyes, he saw the form of the old engineer. The seat-box had turned over, wedged against the boilerhead, pinning him to the slanted deck.

Slade seized it, put forth his full strength and tore it free. He seized the body of the unconscious engineer and edged back to the gangway, flame searing his flesh, smoke and steam filling his lungs. His head reeled, red flashes stormed before his eyes. His chest seemed bursting; he knew he was going fast. Should he lose his grip, both he and the old hogger would perish. He redoubled his efforts as his strength ebbed.

Shouts from outside. He realized that hands reached to him as his feet dangled out the gangway. With a final effort, summoning his remaining strength, he lunged back, gulped a deep draft of life-giving air. Hands seized him, and the engineer and he were hauled to safety amid cheers from the bruised and shaken passengers who had streamed from the coaches.

In the fresh air, his strength quickly returned. Slade examined the engineer, who was already muttering with returning consciousness, and concluded his hurt was not serious.

"Lump on his noggin from where it was rammed against the boilerhead, knocking him out, that's all," was his verdict. "Fire didn't get to him."

"Thanks to you," said the fireman whose injuries, though painful, were also superficial. "If it wasn't for you he would have been roasted."

The baggage master had crawled from his overturned car. The express messenger, gun in hand, was peering cautiously out the door. Both had suffered some contusions, not bad. Nor were any passengers badly hurt.

"Lucky we'd slowed up a bit for the curve," observed the fireman. "And Tom saw the rail was missing in time to shut the throttle and set the brakes before we hit. Otherwise it would have been worse."

Slade agreed, but felt the mess was enough to cause a wreck train foreman to lose his mind.

"There's the rail over there by the brush, and the wrench and spike puller used to remove it," he said. He turned to the blue clad conductor who was hovering about.

"Have you a portable telegraph instrument aboard?" he asked. "You should have one."

"Yes, we've got one," replied the conductor. "I can tap out enough to tell Sanderson what happened, but I don't see how we are going to hook it up," with a dubious glance at the tall telegraph pole beside the right-of-way.

"Fetch the instrument, I'll hook it up,"

145

Slade told him.

Meanwhile, Crane was examining the bodies of the slain wreckers.

"Shot to pieces," he announced. "Nope, don't remember seein' the devils before."

The conductor returned with the instrument. Slade went up the pole like a squirrel, to the accompaniment of admiring exclamations. He hooked up the wires. The conductor began tapping.

"Okay," he called, a few minutes later. "They're on their way."

Slade cast loose the wires and threw them to the ground, then slid down the pole. Securing his medicaments, he patched up the fireman's cuts and attended to a couple of passengers.

"That should hold you for the time being," he said. Leaning against the pole, he rolled and lighted a cigarette.

"We'll stick around until the wreck train arrives," he decided. "Looks like, after all, that the contractors and their men will receive their money in time. We'll pack it aboard the train that will be sent to convey the passengers to town."

"Uh-huh, thanks to you and your hunches," said Crane. "Never knew 'em to fail."

Slade examined the point where the rail

had been removed and arrived at a certain conclusion.

"Very, very smart," he said to the sheriff. "The cunning devil never overlooks the smallest detail. He heaped earth and cinders to produce a fair simulacrum of a rail, so that the engineer wouldn't note its absence in time, not giving a hang how many people might be killed in the wreck."

"That's right," broke in the engineer, who was sitting up puffing on his pipe. "I didn't catch on that there was no iron there until I was right on top of it.

"And, son," he added, "I reckon I owe my worthless old carcass to you. If you hadn't risked your own life to haul me out, I'd got a taste of fire before my time. Much obliged!"

"It was a pleasure to be able to lend a hand," Slade smiled.

"Pleasure!" snorted the hogger. "Crawlin' through smoke and fire and hot steam! I got another name for it."

"That reminds me," said the sheriff. "Get me that jar of salve from your pouch."

Despite Slade's protests that it wasn't necessary, he smeared his face with the soothing ointment.

"Should keep you from blistering," he said, capping the jar and handing it back.

"Want your gal to give me hell for not looking after you? Betcha she'll be in town tomorrow, after word gets to the spread of this shindig."

Smoke was rising beyond the curve. Trainmen hurried forward to learn the details of what happened.

"Everything westbound tied up," remarked the sheriff. "Guess they'll hold the eastbound stuff at Sanderson. Well, this makes twice you've tangled train robber twine in this section."

"And I hope it will be the last," Slade replied. "Only a Heaven's blessing that somebody wasn't killed this time."

"Plus you being on the job at just the right time," said Crane. "Guess even Heaven above can use a helping hand down here now and then."

The wreck train roared in, an engine with a couple of coaches to accommodate the stranded passengers who followed it. The money was transferred from the express car safe. The messenger sat beside it with a gun in his hand. Sheriff Crane assigned the two deputies to keep him company, just in case. He and Slade would bring their horses to town.

The bodies of the outlaws were also loaded onto the Sanderson train. The rigs were removed from the horses they had ridden, which were found tethered in the brush, and the animals turned loose to fend for themselves until picked up.

Followed by praise and congratulations, and the repeated fervent thanks of the engineer, Slade and the sheriff headed for Sanderson. With them rode old Doc Cooper, forking Deputy Blount's mount, who had arrived with the wreck train. Looking over Slade's ministrations, he declared profanely that there hadn't been any sense in bothering him. He did examine a few passengers who had suffered minor cuts from flying glass and applied a little court plaster.

"Young hellion sure missed his calling when he didn't decide to become a doctor," he declared, apropos of Slade. "He's got a touch, and surgeon's hands, and no nerves, and don't guzzle too blasted much redeye."

"Yep, that's his only fault," said Crane. "Coffee! Sometime he'll turn into a coffee bush with nice white flowers. Speed up, I'm hungry!"

Sanderson was wild with excitement when they reached the railroad town, long after dark. The train had arrived first and the deputies and the passengers had spread the story around. When Slade and the sheriff entered the Branding Pen, a cheer arose that quivered the hanging lamps and they were mobbed by admirers, until the sheriff bawled,

"Scatter, all you horned toads! We're plumb starved and hanker for a surrounding. Yes, the carcasses are at my office. Come around later and look 'em over. Now we aim to eat."

Hardrock added his voice and the two law enforcement officers were allowed to enjoy their meal in peace. The sheriff topped it off with a double snort, Slade with an extra cup of coffee and a cigarette. For a while they sat silent in full-fed content, each busy with his own thoughts. Crane abruptly broke into speech,

"I've a notion the devils are getting a mite frantic about now, don't you think?"

"I imagine they are experiencing a slight disquietude," Slade agreed.

"Wonder how many of them are left?"

"Well, we know there are four," Slade said. "No telling for sure how many more, if any. But of the four, there is no doubt but that one is the leader of the pack and someone to reckon with."

"You're right there," Crane growled. "The way he wrecked that train was plumb smart and plumb devilish; might have killed fifty people, if those coaches had turned over."

"Which would not have bothered him in the least," Slade replied. "He has absolutely no regard for the sanctity of human life. As clever and snake-blooded a character as we have ever been up against. Reminds me of Veck Sosna, and perhaps even smarter. Sosna's weakness was personal vanity, while I've a notion this hellion takes himself for granted and doesn't care the slightest what others think of him and has no desire to make an impression on others. Sufficient unto himself. Which is arrogance at its worst."

"I reckon, whatever the devil that means," Crane agreed. "Anyhow, he's a sidewinder for fair, and just like a sidewinder, strikes without any warning. Oh, well, his time will come; he'll try to gang once too often."

"Hope you're right," Slade said, smilingly. "Meanwhile, he still packs plenty of poison. Seems when I'm thinking I've been up against the worst character of my experience, along comes another that tops him. Of course, as I've said before, examples of the new type of criminal invading the West, introducing big city methods. Just as salty as the old-time brush popper, but with more brains."

Hardrock Hogan came over to join them

and the discussion was dropped. The owner sat down and ordered drinks.

"Fletcher Bartlett and his hands were here a little while ago," he announced. "Said they figured it was safe to leave the spread to take care of itself, seeing as Mr. Slade has cleaned up the wide-loopers, and decided they could stand a spell in town, it being Saturday night and things lively."

"His optimism may be a trifle premature," Slade said.

"I doubt it," Hardrock rejoined cheerfully. "Just wait till he hears about the attempted train robbery and how it was busted up, if he hasn't already heard it. He'll be rarin' to go. Said he'd be back here a little later. And you sure have made a change in that wind spider, Mr. Slade. 'Pears to have turned into a real nice feller."

"I've a notion he always was, at the bottom, only was sort of ashamed to show it. Wanted to set up as a tough hombre," Slade said.

"And you sure took him down a peg," chuckled Hardrock. "Guess that's what he needed. Drink hearty, gents; another one coming up."

Still chuckling, he ambled back to the far end of the bar to attend to chores, for now the usual Saturday night activities were getting under way and the Branding Pen was filling up.

Sheriff Crane regarded Slade curiously. "Well," he said, "looks like that counts Bartlett out so far as the train robbery was concerned. He could hardly be in two places at once."

"He has been counted out for quite a while," Slade replied smilingly.

"And he ain't the jigger you've had an eye on?"

"He certainly is not, nor has he been for some time," Slade said.

"Then who the devil have you had your eye on?" Crane demanded exasperatedly.

"The real trouble maker, the head of the wolf pack," Slade replied. "Glen Graham."

Fourteen

The sheriff stared incredulously.

"You don't mean it!"

"I do," Slade answered.

"But — but —" sputtered the bewildered peace officer, "you never seemed to pay any attention to him."

"More than you thought, from the time I first met him, in your office," Slade said.

"But why in the office?"

"Because he lied."

"Lied?"

"Yes. You will recall that he came in, ostensibly, to report stolen stock."

"That's right," the sheriff agreed.

"And he said that the cattle were lifted from around a big waterhole on the southeast reach of his land and that he presumed they were run across Fletcher Bartlett's holding," Slade resumed. "He said there was no tracking them because of the heavy grass. I'm familiar with that section of the range, having, as you know, ridden over it a number of times. I know that waterhole. It's the only one in the vicinity, which is why the cows gather around it. The grass there is not heavy. It is sparse, very sparse, in fact, for a mile or so to the south and east, because of some soil deficiency. Any cowhand could have easily tracked cows across it. Graham deliberately lied when he said otherwise. And when a man lies for no apparent reason, I become interested.

"The truth is, Graham didn't lose any stock, although he reported he had."

"But why in blazes did he do it?" asked Crane.

"To cast suspicion on Fletcher Bartlett who was already under suspicion in certain quarters; you leaned that way yourself. Bartlett came in handy for Graham, furthering his aims."

"Well, I'll be hanged!" exploded the sheriff. "The way you point it out, it does look sorta funny. What else?"

"Remember the drygulching attempted against Pancho Arista on the Marathon trail. Without a doubt, somebody rode ahead of Arista to make the try. Graham was with you in the office when Arista told you of his intention. Nobody else knew about it. Nobody, not even the bank people, knew what Arista intended to do with the money he drew from his account. He's a secretive cuss, but I suppose he felt safe in talking with you and figuring that Graham was all right because he was here with you in the office and to all appearances quite friendly with you. Anyhow, he talked.

"So only you and Graham knew what he had in mind. Graham, of course, sensed an opportunity to make a good haul. He dispatched one of his devils ahead of Arista, who didn't leave town until an hour or more after he talked with you, to set the trap."

"And if it hadn't been for you and your flash-lightning ways of figuring things, it would have worked," growled Crane.

"Possibly," Slade conceded. "Anyhow, it fixed my attention firmly on Graham. From that moment on there was no doubt in my mind but Graham was my man. But proving it was something else again. I still can't prove anything against him. I have never gotten a look at him that would enable me to swear the man I saw indulging in criminal acts was Glen Graham."

"Anything else?" Crane asked.

"His buying into Tumulty's saloon had me curious, and puzzled, for a while," Slade continued. "Until I realized it provided him with a perfect set-up. He could meet with his men there, consult with them, outline his plans and dispatch them on whatever missions he had in mind, with nobody thinking anything of it. He talked with all the customers, especially new ones, which was what is expected from a bar owner. He couldn't meet with them at his ranch house, because that would have caused his legitimate hands to grow curious and wonder what it was all about. So he hit on the method I outlined, and it was a good one."

Slade paused to roll and light a cigarette, then resumed:

"You will recall that Tumulty immediately recognized the bodies of the owlhoots we brought in as men who had been in his place and, he was pretty sure, talked with Graham. I'm willing to wager that he'll also remember as being in his bar the three we

156

brought in tonight."

"How about those two fellers we wondered about for a time, who drygulched the drunk from the alley?" Crane asked.

"I'm still not exactly sure about them," Slade replied. "But I have a feeling that they were two of the four that escaped tonight, and that probably the fellow with a short leg, who gunned the talkative drunk from the alley is the third, the fourth being Graham himself. Does he have any more on tap? I wish I knew for sure."

"And do you figure he's got you spotted as a Ranger?"

"I doubt it," Slade said. "I think he's just got me tagged as El Halcon, a known trouble maker and with a reputation of horning in on good things others have started, who manages to pull the wool over the eyes of stupid sheriffs."

"I'll pull the wool over his eyes, or watch somebody pull earth over 'm with a spade," vowed the sheriff. "Yes, you've sure made out a case against the devil, without anything more."

"And with no proof with which to back it up," Slade reminded him.

"So we've got to get the sidewinder dead to rights," growled Crane.

"Sure looks that way," Slade agreed.

"Incidentally, I feel he made a slip when he borrowed money from the business. As we agreed, he must be getting short of ready cash, having had little luck with his hoped-for hauls of late. That, in a way, substantiated my diagnosis of the case."

"It sure did," agreed the sheriff. "And you figure he'll pull something else soon?"

"He certainly will," Slade answered. "And we can hardly hope for another such lucky break as in the case of the attempted train robbery. Had it not been for those box cars turning over on the faulty lead, I wouldn't have known the Flyer was packing that money. Or at least not soon enough. It was Peleg Sutton's chance remark, when he said jokingly that he hoped the Flyer wouldn't turn over on the way here like the cars did, that informed me of the fact in time for us to get organized and tangle the devil's twine for him. Another example of the importance of trifles, or what seem to be trifles."

"And which you never overlook," said Crane. "Well, I've a strong notion his 'trifling' is just about over."

"Hope you're right," Slade replied smilingly.

Said the sheriff, "Let us drink!"

And they did. Slade coffee, the sheriff a snort of redeye.

Crane shoved his empty glass aside and glanced at the clock.

"Reckon we'd better get back to the office for a spell," he suggested. "Chances are somebody will want to look at the carcasses."

Several somebodies did, with negative results. Slade sent a deputy to fetch George Tumulty. When the bar owner arrived, his reactions were what the Ranger expected them to be.

"Yep, they were all three in my place, yesterday or day before, I don't remember which. Yep, I wouldn't be surprised if Graham talked with them; he talks with everybody. Maybe he'll remember something about them."

Slade thought Graham very probably would, but would be highly unlikely to divulge it.

Not that he expected the GG owner would drop in; he believed Graham would steer clear of the sheriff's office in the immediate future.

"Well, I figure it's bedtime," Crane said, after Tumulty departed. "I'm beginning to feel a mite weary; been a busy day."

"A notion," Slade agreed. "I can stand a session of ear pounding. See you tomorrow, later today, rather, it's long past midnight."

As Crane predicted, old John Webb and Mary Merril rode to get particulars about the train robbery attempt. They had dinner with Slade and the sheriff at the Branding Pen. After they had finished eating, Peleg Sutton, the railroad yardmaster and maintenance superintendent, entered. Slade waved him to join them. He was introduced and accepted a chair and a drink. Old John wandered to the bar to speak with some cronies. A little later he called Slade to corroborate something. Sutton's eyes followed the Ranger, curiously.

"A deputy sheriff!" he remarked. "A rather humble calling for a man of his ability."

"Yes," Mary said gently, "but to a humble fisherman was given The Keys of the Kingdom!"

Peleg Sutton, a man thoroughly grounded in the Scriptures, bowed his head.

FIFTEEN

Several peaceful days followed. If Glen Graham planned to pull something, he was certainly in no rush about it. Slade, however, experienced a mounting disquietude. He and the sheriff racked their brains in an endeavor to anticipate just where the cunning devil would strike, but no success.

160

"Any day, now," El Halcon said. "And it will be something devilish and ingenious, you can depend on that. Very likely somewhere we aren't thinking about."

As usual, Slade was right.

Running south from Marathon into the wild fastnesses of the Big Bend is a trail. It is an old trail. Venturesome Spaniards rode it to reach the Trans-Pecos mountains, where they expected to find gold and silver. The Comanches travelled it on their way to raid into Mexico. Smugglers rode it, and still ride it, as do outlaws headed for Marathon, Sanderson, Alpine, and other points east and west.

It continues toward the dim blue bulk of distant mountains. Santiago Peak, loftiest summit of the Santiago Range, lifts its rocky head into the blue of the Texas sky. Caballo Mountain is visible. The Santiago Chain, a part of the broken backbone of the Rockies, looms ahead. It flows through Persimmon Gap, where it is known locally as the Comanche Trail, blazed by raiding Indians from the South Plains, it is said, although the trail is far older than the Comanches. Then on and on past the Chisos Mountains, Dogie Mountain, and Willow Mountain, and to Terlingua, one of the largest quicksilver deposits in the world.

161

And from Terlingua, northbound, came carts loaded with the containers of quicksilver, headed for Marathon and a buyer.

Quicksilver is very valuable and there is a good market for it, so the two big carts were guarded. Three outriders accompanied them, keen, alert men chosen for courage and skill with rifle and sixgun.

The carts started north before daybreak and, each drawn by four sturdy mules, travelled fast. A night camp was made and the outriders stood guard in shifts during the hours of darkness. Again with the first flush of dawn they continued on their way, hoping and expecting to reach Marathon before nightfall.

Through the wild and lonely country to the south the outriders were very watchful, not expecting trouble but taking no chances. They breathed easier when they reached Persimmon Gap and rolled through it without incident. Now the way was fairly open and peaceful and before long, they were but a few miles from Marathon. The outriders relaxed still more, bunched behind the carts, for the trail was narrow.

Suddenly they raised their heads and became vigilant. From beyond a bend flanked by brush came a click of horses' irons and voices raised in raucous whoops and equally raucous singing. Around the bend bulged five riders, swaying in their saddles, yelling and singing at the top of their voices. One waved a bottle. The outriders failed to note or attach any significance to the fact that he waved it with his left hand.

The guards relaxed again, chuckling. Just a bunch of cowhands returning from a spree in town.

The five riders bawled a greeting.

"Here, fellers, have a snort!" bellowed the one with the bottle. The guards smilingly shook their heads.

Up to the carts surged the apparently well fortified horsemen, weaving aside as if to pass the train, slowing their mounts.

Without warning, their hands flickered down and up. The air quivered to a roar of gunfire.

The guards tried to fight back, but caught unprepared and utterly surprised, they never had a chance. Two, and one of the cartmen, went down under that first murderous volley. The one remaining managed to fire a single shot before he fell to lie motionless in the dust. The second cart driver died at almost the same instant.

The startled and confused mules halted. The carts came to a standstill.

One of the killers, a tall and broad-shouldered man, heavily bearded, snapped an order. Two changed from their horses to the cart seats. The bearded man and his companion swiftly went through their victims' pockets, transferring money to their own. The bearded man exclaimed with satisfaction as he drew forth an invoice sheet that listed the contents of the carts and the expected payment, a large sum.

The carts moved on toward Marathon, behind them the five bodies lying in the trail, the three wondering horses ridden by the guards standing beside them.

Shortly after sunset, the carts reached Marathon, but before they entered the town, the led horses belonging to the pair driving the carts were concealed in a dense thicket less than a mile from the outskirts.

The bearded man, evidently the leader of the band, a courteous and affable individual, knew exactly where to locate the buyer and called him by name.

The buyer had no reason to believe everything was not as it should be. The bearded man appeared perfectly familiar with his business. He mentioned the name of the manager of the Terlingua mine — the well known Chisos Mine — and other details as he presented the invoice. The buyer checked the contents of the carts and without hesitation paid over the money for the shipment which he had been impatiently awaiting in order to fulfill certain commitments he had made. He pointed out a stable where the mules and the horses would be cared for. Neither he nor anybody else noted that the two men who had driven the carts mounted behind two of the supposed to be cart guards and the devilish bunch rode swiftly to the thicket where the two horses were concealed, retrieved them and continued east at a fast pace.

However, as it happened, one of the cart guards was not dead, although he had received a bad head wound and to all appearances was done for. At least, so the outlaws evidently thought and neglected to fire another slug into his body.

But many hours elapsed and he recovered consciousness. Weak, dizzy but with grim courage, he managed to mount his horse, a well trained beast that had remained close to its rider's body, and finally reached Marathon with the story of the outrage.

Sheriff Traynor was notified. He sent a wire to Sheriff Crane at Sanderson, which Crane received after more delay. He and Slade and the deputies rode west on the Marathon trail for some miles, against the faint chance that they might meet the out-laws.

After a while Slade called a halt. "We're just wasting time and energy," he said. "Chances are the devils reached Sanderson some time ago or turned off somewhere. This time Graham put it over nicely. Oh, sure, the one wearing the false beard was Graham, and very likely the others also displayed a fair growth of bristles. Clean shaven, it's doubtful that the buyer would be able to positively identify them even if he got the chance to look them over, which is highly improbable. Back to town! We should get more details of what happened tomorrow. Yes, chalk one up for his side."

"Anyhow, it didn't happen in my baili-wick," remarked Crane.

"But definitely in mine," Slade replied. "And now the hellion is well supplied with cash and may lay off for a while and give us another period of guessing. Then again, however, his confidence in himself restored and the morale of his men raised, he may strike again and with little delay. Well, we'll see."

The following afternoon Sheriff Traynor came to Sanderson, via train, and they received the details of the outrage as supplied by the buyer and the wounded cart guard, who was recovering.

"The devil must have been planning that one for some time," was Slade's comment. "Thoroughly familiarized himself with all the angles both in Terlingua and Marathon. No trouble for him to learn when a shipment was expected. And his method of drygulching the cart train was unique, and effective by its very simplicity."

"The nerve of the sidewinder, bringing the stuff to town and selling it to the man who was supposed to buy it," growled Traynor.

"Simplicity again," Slade replied. "And about the only way he could have hoped to dispose of it. Could hardly hope to drive a couple of loaded carts around while he hunted up an illicit purchaser. Oh, he's something very much in the nature of a genius. Better keep an eye on your office safe, Chet, or he'll be carting it off under your nose."

"Wouldn't surprise me one bit," conceded Traynor. "Or kidnap me and hold me for ransom. Ain't nothing safe so long as he's on the loose. What next! What next!"

"Your question," Slade smiled. "You find the answer."

"I ain't got an answer to anything," snorted Traynor. "I'll admit it, I'm plumb buffaloed."

"And that goes double for me," growled Crane.

Slade chuckled. He felt he was in something of the same condition as the despondent sheriffs. Glen Graham was definitely in the driver's seat. He knew exactly what he intended to do, while Slade could only guess. Well, maybe the wind spider would make the wrong turn and upset the whole shebang. Had happened that way before when to all appearances he was completely baffled. In the words of Dickens' Mr. Micawber, something would always turn up.

While this was comforting to dwell on, it was not exactly dependable and he feared it would be up to him to give the "turning" a slight boost. He rolled a cigarette and he and the sheriffs conned over possibilities that could prove attractive to an outlaw. The banks at Ozone and McCame were mentioned.

"When Crater Moral was operating in the section when you were here the last time, he hit both those banks, you'll remember," remarked Crane.

"And announced himself as Crater Moral," put in Traynor. "Got so folks shivered at mention of the name. Well, you did for Moral, just as you finally did for

Juan Covelo, who was a hyderphobia skunk if there ever was one. I figure Graham is going to end up just the same way. Yep, end up with his toes up."

"Thanks for your confidence," Slade said smilingly. "Hope you're right. Sometimes I believe Graham is worse than either of those varmints — more brains. Just as ruthless and bloodthirsty but with an intelligence that surpasses theirs. The hardest sort on which to drop a loop."

"Swing it wide," chuckled Crane. "Haul in the whole bunch. Gents, I'm hungry."

"You always are," grunted Traynor. "Oh, all right, let's go eat. Guess the Branding Pen is your favorite stuffin' and guzzlin' joint, yes?"

They found the Branding Pen busy and noisy as usual. Several persons, including Hardrock Hogan, dropped over to discuss the cart robbery and gather details from Traynor, and departed shaking their heads at the daring and ingenuity displayed by the robbers.

While the sheriffs talked, Slade concentrated mentally on the problem that confronted him, with scant results. It was like trying to hold water in the clenched hand; the harder one grasps it, the easier it slips away.

Finally, in disgust, he gave up the whole perplexing business, banishing it from his mind until inspiration should take a notion to come along.

The sheriffs ambled to the bar to commune with some acquaintance. Slade was left alone with his thoughts. Abruptly, he stiffened slightly in his chair. Two men had entered and made their way to the middle of the bar, seeming perfectly at their ease, evincing no perturbation as they stood sipping their drinks and conversing together.

They were the pair who had left the saloon on payday night, shortly before the drunken babbler was gunned down from the alley, Slade's on-again-off-again suspects, but whom he was now firmly convinced were two of the remaining members of Glen Graham's outlaw bunch. To all appearances, they didn't have a care in the world.

Well, it wasn't strange, Slade thought. He believed they did not think that he suspected them of anything. Or at least that he had nothing on them. Which was unpleasantly close to the truth. He wondered if their visit to the Branding Pen had been casual, or had they something in mind. If so, he'd doubtless learn about it soon enough, and it wouldn't be pleasant.

And then inspiration arrived. In the very

portly person of Cruikshanks, the Hog Wallow owner, who waddled in for a gab with Hardrock, who, at that moment, was keeping Slade company while the sheriffs were at the bar. He greeted Slade, accepted a drink, and eased himself cautiously into a chair.

"Well, how's the freighting business?" Hogan asked.

Cruikshanks, who was quite mellow, per usual, took no particular pains to keep his voice down.

"Gettin' out of it as fast as I can," he said. "Plumb tired of being bothered. Only got a few wagons going, that I haven't been able to dispose of yet. Sent one up to that little scattering of houses they call Comanche, on the Pecos trail and this side of Fort Stockton, loaded with stuff including some machinery for a feller who owns a ranch close to there. Coming back empty 'cept for a sorta hefty poke of dinero he got from the sale of a herd and wants deposited in the Sanderson bank. Nope, I ain't looking for new business. Doing the jigger a favor, in a way, packing his money along. Just can't be bothered any more. Wagon should be here in the evening tomorrow, and then it goes into storage; I'm through."

Slade listened in silence while Cruik-

171

shanks rambled on concerning the disadvantages of the freighting business that interrupted a man's drinking. He wondered what other ears might also be listening.

However, although his brows drew together, he did not remonstrate with the Hog Wallow owner for his lack of discretion. To do so would have sounded silly, and Cruikshanks was in no condition to listen to reason.

A little later, the two men who had attracted Slade's attention shoved their empty glasses aside and departed. They did not glance toward the table. While the two bar owners chattered on, Slade sat very, very thoughtful.

The two men could hardly have missed overhearing the Hog Wallow owner's bumbling remarks. And there was no doubt at all but that Graham would sense opportunity and very likely react accordingly.

And Slade believed opportunity might well be provided for him also.

He pondered taking the sheriffs into his confidence, but decided against it, believing he would have a better chance of success by himself. Better to play a lone hand, even with the odds heavily against him and the grave personal danger to which he gave little thought. The element of surprise would be in his favor, as well as the terrain over which the money wagon must pass. He might well be able to get the jump on the scoundrels and, with a little luck, clean out the whole nest of varmints. Worth giving a whirl, anyhow. Of course nothing might come of it, but a hunch was beginning to make itself felt. He'd play it.

Sixteen

Slade knew that for forty miles south of the tiny pueblo of Comanche, little more than a name, the trail ran past ranches, worming its way through draws and arroyos that were treacherous during wet weather. There were low ridges, thick stands of brush, deep gullys. All in all, an inviting terrain for a drygulching.

He believed it logical to assume that if the bunch did contemplate a raid on the wagon, they would pull it no great distance from Sanderson. Then, by circling around to the west, they could reach the town with a minimum risk of being detected, especially after dusk. Yes, that was very likely how they'd work it were they really to make a try.

Cruikshanks said goodnight and lumbered out. Slade watched him go, wondering at the carelessness of people. Of course the whole affair was of minor importance to the Hog Wallow owner. The money involved meant little to him, and apparently he never thought that if the outlaws did strike his wagon, the driver would very likely be murdered.

Indeed, it was doubtful if it had ever dawned on him that the wagon might be the object of an owlhoot raid.

The sheriffs returned to the table. Traynor glanced at the clock.

"Getting late," he said. "Me, I'm going to bed."

"Me, too," replied Crane. "How about you, Walt?"

"I'm heading for the Regan House as soon as I finish my coffee," Slade said evasively.

For a short while after the pair left, he sat on, smoking a cigarette and sipping coffee. Shoving his empty cup aside, he left the Branding Pen and did make his way to the hotel. In his room, he sat down by the open window, without lighting the lamp, and went over the plan he had been building up in his mind. A very good plan, he thought, if he could just put it properly into execution.

For a little less than an hour he sat by the window, smoking and thinking, while the noise in the street subsided with only a die-hard reveller now and then passing by the hotel. He glanced out the window, extinguished his cigarette butt and quietly left the room. At the lobby door he paused a moment, searching the street with his eyes. There was nobody in sight.

Walking swiftly, he reached Shadow's stable and quickly cinched up.

"Chance to stretch your legs a mite," he told the big black. "Reckon you can stand it."

Shadow, who detested inaction, tossed his head and blew through his nose.

Upon reaching the trail, Slade rode east at a moderate gait, constantly scanning the back trail, upon which there was no sign of life. After some miles, confident that if anybody had been keeping tabs on his movements, the maneuver had deceived them, he turned and rode back west at a fast pace, turning into the Pecos trail that ran north by a veering to the west. Again he watched the back trail for a while, then faced to the front.

The stars were brilliant in a purple sky and large objects were visible for quite some distance. A lonesome little wind wandered through the grassheads as if uncertain where to go. The only sound that broke the great hush was the far-off yipping of a couple of coyotes. The general effect was unreal, and a trifle eerie, as if nature were holding its breath in anticipation of coming events. Or so it seemed to El Halcon's vivid imagination; and the hunch was growing stronger.

For some miles he continued at a steady pace. Around the water holes he passed, cattle lay contentedly chewing their cuds, rolling great wondering eyes at the lone horseman, and giving vent to an occasional disapproving snort, as if resenting his disturbing presence. Slade chuckled, and rode on.

Before long he reached broken ground, where the arroyos were deep, the ridges clothed with tall chaparral. After a bit, he turned from the trail and made his way down the side of a dry wash. As he expected, there was grass on the floor of the wash, and clumps of thicket. Removing the rig, he turned Shadow loose to graze, supplementing his diet with a couple of handfuls of oats from a saddle pouch. Then, just inside the edge of the thicket, he rolled up in his blanket with his saddle for a pillow and quickly was sound asleep, not awakening until well past daybreak.

He was in no hurry, for he knew the

wagon from Comanche would not reach the vicinity until the afternoon was well along. So, from staple provisions in his saddle pouches he cooked a satisfying breakfast over a tiny fire of dry wood that gave off a minimum of smoke.

After eating, and cleaning up the utensils, he rolled a cigarette and pondered his next move. Being familiar with the trail and its surroundings, he had a fairly good notion as to about where the try for the wagon would be made, if one really was made, and believed that certain physical features of the terrain would work to his advantage.

In fact there was but one spot a little farther on that would be suited to a drygulching. He felt confident the outlaws would not make their attempt at a greater distance from where he was holed up at present. The trail was travelled and there was no turning off from it until the open ground to the south was reached. They would certainly not desire to meet anybody before they were able to circle to the west where there was scant chance of being noted. So the area he had in mind would undoubtedly be the reasonable choice.

Knowing it would still be many hours before the wagon would put in an appearance, he stretched out on his blanket and drowsed for a while longer, comfortable in the warm sunshine. The air, with Autumn well on the way, had a tangy nip that rendered the sun warmth desirable.

Shadow, his belly well lined, stood with head hanging and eyes closed, evidently enjoying a snooze. But Slade knew that if anybody approached the wash he would instantly be wide awake and aware of their approach even before the remarkable hearing of El Halcon would catch the sound.

So his master drowsed free from apprehension, sleepily conning over the details of his plan to thwart any attempt on the money wagon and, with a little luck, perhaps bag himself an owlhoot or two. This was not altogether beyond reason, if he didn't turn out to be the bagged instead of the bagger. Well, he'd just have to take his chances.

Finally, he glanced at the sun, which had crossed the zenith, stood up, yawned, stretched and replaced the rig, making sure that his high-power Winchester was smooth in the boot, his big Colts in their sheaths. Mounting, he rode out of the wash and continued along the almost straight trail with no encroaching brush, as was the condition until the open range was reached.

But a mile or so to the north the picture changed. Growth edged against the track on both sides, with a couple of hundred yards above the crest of a ridge.

However, he quickly realized that the spot was not as ideal for the possible drygulchers as he had thought. Several nights of frost had stripped most of the leaves from the chaparral at the foot of the ridge. On the crest was a different type of growth which had not been so much affected by the low temperature.

"Which makes it better for us, feller," he told Shadow. "If the hellions do hole up here as I believe they will, we'll be able to spot them from the ridge top, while we should be pretty well hidden, which should work to our advantage. Okay, up you go and stop fussing; you've tackled worse than this without cracking your blasted neck."

Shadow's reply, were it translated, would not have looked well in print. However, they reached the crest without accident and holed up comfortably, from where they had a clear view of the trail with little chance of themselves being detected.

Now there was nothing to do but wait, and a long and tiresome wait it proved to be, without a sign of the outlaws. And as the hours passed and the sun sank in the west, Slade grew acutely uneasy. It began to look like his hunch wasn't a straight one. If the devils had something planned they would surely have put in an appearance before now. Well, maybe any minute and they'd show to take up positions close to the trail.

They didn't. And Slade experienced a feeling of frustration and disgust.

Then abruptly, he straightened in the saddle as Shadow blew softly through his nose. A sound had come riding the wings of the wind, a low mutter that steadily increased in volume until it was a rumble. A wagon was rolling down from the north, very like Cruikshank's freighting wagon. For the moment it was obscured by a brush-flanked bend in the trail less than a hundred yards beyond where Slade sat on his horse.

Another moment and it rounded the bend into view. Yes, it was a big freighter with only one man on the driver's seat. Slade relaxed, watched it pass to toil up the long slope to the south.

"So our hunch fluffed out," he remarked to Shadow. "But we'll amble along behind that shebang, just in case."

He sent Shadow down the slope to the trail. Just as he reached it, he straightened again. Another sound had smote his ears. A sharp clicking, the beat of fast hoofs on the surface of the trail, coming from the north.

He turned Shadow to face in that direction, leaned forward, tense, every sense at hair-trigger alertness.

Around the bend bulged four horsemen travelling at a rapid pace. They sighted him the instant he sighted them. Startled exclamations arose. They jerked to a halt, went for their guns. Slade whipped the Winchester from the boot.

The best defense, with the odds against him, was offense. Weaving, ducking in the saddle, he sent Shadow charging forward.

Straight into the blaze of gunfire he rode, the Winchester flaming. Answering slugs buzzed around him, ripped his sleeve, tore through the crown of his hat, grazed the flesh of his thigh.

A man whirled from the saddle as if struck by a sledgehammer blow. A second reeled back. The grip of his dying hands tightened on the reins and his horse reared up and up on its hind legs, strove to catch its balance, and fell in a kicking tangle. The remaining pair whirled their mounts and streaked back for the bend. Slade lined sights — and the hammer clicked on an empty shell. With an oath, he slammed the rifle into the boot. His voice rang out,

"Trail, Shadow, trail!"

Forward bounded the great black, almost

reached the bend. But at that instant, the fallen horse lunged to its feet squarely in front of him. No chance to swerve. He hit the other cayuse shoulder to shoulder and knocked it sprawling.

But he was right on top of it. He stumbled, lurched over its body and fell headlong. Slade just had time to free his feet from the stirrups. Then he was flying through the air to hit the ground with terrific force.

For minutes he lay gasping and writhing, flashes storming before his eyes, his head whirling. He felt as if every bone in his body were broken. He tried to rise, almost got to his knees and fell back. His lungs seemed drained of air, his throat choked. More minutes passed before he did manage to stagger erect to stand weaving. Thankfully he sensed that no bones were actually broken, although they felt that way. Gradually his mind cleared. His coordination approached normal.

The horses had also regained their footing and stood glaring daggers at one another and voicing equine profanity.

"*You* were to blame for this trouble, you blankety-blank-blank!" their indignant snorts seemed to say.

"Never mind who's to blame, the fact remains the hellion escaped," Slade told them. "I'm willing to swear the taller one was Graham, but I couldn't swear it in court. Never got anything like a good look at his face, through powder smoke and at that distance. Well, anyhow, we managed to tie onto a couple of the devils, which isn't too bad; something to pack to town with us."

Rolling a cigarette with fingers that still shook a little, he contemplated with satisfaction the two bodies sprawled in the dust.

The first to fall under the hammerings of the Winchester slugs he recognized as one of the pair who had intrigued him from the first, who left the Branding Pen shortly after Cruikshanks' unguarded remarks the night before. He approached the other body, straightened it out. Yes, the hellion who drygulched the talkative drunk from the alley mouth across from the Branding Pen; one leg was distinctly shorter than the other. No, not too bad.

Just the same, however, he felt he had been nicely outsmarted. As usual, Graham had done the unexpected. He never missed a bet. Instead of holing up in the sparse growth and waiting for the wagon to show, the outlaws had ridden well to the north, presumably the night before, then holed up in comfort during the day. When they sighted the distant wagon coming down from the north, they left their hiding place. Then, not wishing to pull the drygulching far from the open rangeland, they rode south, allowing the swiftly moving vehicle to pass their slow-pacing horses, doubtless shouting jovial greetings to their intended victim. They followed, keeping their distance.

When the wagon neared the base of the long slope, breasting which it would slow, they speeded up to overtake it. Then a shot in the driver's back; the money secured; a quick ride to the open ground only a short distance away; a circle to the west, and back to Sanderson with nobody the wiser.

Yes, a complicated maneuver, every detail carefully planned, and very near successful. It was only because of the unexpected appearance of El Halcon that it was not.

Or so Slade interpreted the interrupted plan of action, and believed he was right.

"And if we'd just figured it in advance, and stayed up top, there's a good chance we *would* have bagged the sidewinder," he told Shadow. "Oh, well, guess nobody is right all the time, and you and I are no exception to the rule."

He pinched out his cigarette and again approached the bodies.

"We'll load them onto the cayuses they used to ride — the one you knocked galley-west appears to be all right, now that he's caught his breath — and pack them to town with us. Got ourselves a couple of souvenirs, at least."

As Slade expected, they overtook the slower moving wagon before they reached town. The driver, a pleasant-faced elderly man, goggled and gulped.

"For the love of Pete!" he gasped. "I thought I heard guns shootin' somewhere behind me right after I topped the sag back there, but figured it was none of my business and kept going. What in blazes happened?"

Slade told him briefly, feeling he had a right to know. The driver gulped again.

"Holy mackerel!" he exclaimed. "Looks like you saved my carcass for me, and I'm sure much obliged. Say! Seems to me I'd oughta know you. Ain't you Mr. Slade, Sheriff Crane's deputy?"

Slade admitted the fact.

"I knew it," declared the driver. "Couldn't be anybody else. So you did for two of the wind spiders and sent the other two skalley-hootin'! Gentlemen, hush!"

"And," Slade admonished, "you might mention to your boss that it would be a

185

good idea to keep a tighter latigo on his jaw and lower his voice when discussing such matters in a public place."

"He'll hear from me," the old driver replied grimly.

SEVENTEEN

It was well past dark when they arrived at the railroad town. They collected quite an entourage on the way to the sheriff's office.

Aroused by the racket, Sheriff Crane stuck his head out the door. He stared, his jaw dropping.

"I knew it!" he bawled at Slade. "Come in here and explain yourself. The rest of you loafers stay out till I send for you. Estes," he called over his shoulder, "you and Blount come and pack the carcasses in and look after the horses."

The deputies, who had been drinking coffee in the back room, hurried to do his bidding.

"Go with them," Slade told Shadow, who was well acquainted with both.

"Guess I can make it safe to the Hog Waller," said the wagon driver and churrup-ed to his team.

After the bodies were carried in and placed on the floor, Crane locked the door and turned expectantly to Slade.

"Get you some coffee first, though," he said. "Okay, here you are. Now let's have it."

Slade told him, in detail, starting with the night before.

"When those two devils left the Branding Pen, I had a very good notion they were taking word to Graham of what Cruikshanks said," he concluded. "So I decided to play another hunch. Was all right so far as it went, but it didn't go far enough. I slipped up and figured wrong."

"I think you did a darn good chore of figurin'," Crane differed. "And you had to go off alone and buck the four of them by yourself! Why in blazes didn't you let me know and I'd have gone with you?"

"Perhaps I should have," Slade admitted. "But I was rather vague in my own mind as to just what I'd do, so concluded to go it myself."

He chuckled. "There on the trail you would have come in handy, especially after Shadow pulled a blooper and I had all the breath knocked out of me. I'm still sore all over."

"And I guess it's up to the county to buy you some more clothes," said Crane, with a glance at his bullet shredded garments.

"Those are sorta airy. Fact is, you're half naked. Well, reckon we might as well let folks in for a look."

The crowd quickly filled the office. The man with the short leg nobody could be sure about, but a number instantly remembered seeing the other in various places, including the Branding Pen.

"Was most of the time another jigger with him," said one informant. "Looked sorta alike, could have been brothers."

"Doubt you'll see that one again," the sheriff remarked dryly. "Okay everybody, out. Come back later if you want to. Slade and me hanker for a surrounding."

"Anything new?" the Ranger asked after the door was closed.

"Nothing, except Mary and old John rode in just before dark," Crane replied. "They're at the Branding Pen. Guess we'd better mosey over there right away. Chances are they're worried. I know I was. You give me the jumps, gallivanting off alone like you do, without saying a word to anybody. Wait while I go through those hellions' pockets, if you haven't."

"Left the chore for you," Slade answered. "Chances are you won't find anything, except maybe some dinero."

The prediction proved correct. Nothing of

interest was discovered, save quite a bit of money, which the sheriff stowed in his safe.

"Part of the quicksilver loot, I reckon," he said.

"Very likely," Slade agreed. "All set? Let's go. I can stand a helping; been quite a while since breakfast."

Without incident, they made their way to the Branding Pen, where they found Webb and Mary Merril anxiously awaiting them. The girl gazed resignedly at Slade's clothes and shook her curly head.

"You look like you'd been crawling through a row of barbed wire fences," she declared.

"Better his duds than his hide," the sheriff returned cheerfully. "Let us drink!"

In reply to their urging, Slade gave a brief resume of his adventurous night and day. Old John growled under his mustache.

"We'll never get the real straight of it out of him," he said. "Makes it sound like the other jiggers just made fool mistakes and he had all the luck. How about it, Mary, figure you can get him to really talk — later?"

"He'll talk!" Miss Merril replied, determinedly. The sheriff chuckled, and drained his glass.

Slade honestly did believe that he got a lucky break in that he was sitting his horse and looking in that direction when the outlaws bulged around the bend and were momentarily thrown off balance by his unexpected materializing before their eyes.

But, blast it! If he'd just had sense enough to remain on the ridge crest a little longer, all the advantage would have been his.

Anyhow, that was the way he felt about it, no matter what the others might think, and blamed himself for his lack of acumen. Oh, heck! He wasn't omniscient and he might as well admit it. He tackled his dinner with the appetite of youth and perfect digestion.

Sam Cruikshanks, the Hog Wallow owner, waddled through the swinging doors and eased himself into a chair. He shook hands with Slade, heartily.

"Guess I'm just a blasted terrapin-brain for sounding off in here like I did last night," he announced. "I never gave it a thought till old Ben Holloway, my driver, told me about it. And did he give me heck and blazes! Been with me for thirty years and speaks his mind just the way he feels about it. Said if it wasn't for you, Mr. Slade, he would have been a gone goslin' because of my quackin' away like a dyin' duck in a thunderstorm. Guess he was right."

Slade was of a similar opinion, but refrained from saying so.

Sheriff Crane glanced about the busy room. "By gosh, how the days roll around!" he suddenly exclaimed. "Do you folks realize tomorrow is payday again? I'd plumb forgot it."

"If you had a bunch of work dodgers to pay off like I have, you wouldn't forget it," grumbled Webb. "Cowhands. Carters! I ain't got two dollars left to rub together in my pocket. Here comes the only horned toad who's gettin' rich. When he walks, his pockets jingle like a flock of bit irons."

He glowered at Hardrock Hogan, who was approaching, rubbing his hands together complacently.

"Heard what you said, Sheriff," he chuckled. "Uh-huh, payday again. Fine! Fine!"

"Fine for you," growled Crane. "But how about me? I'll have to be on my toes all day and all night."

"Oh, Mr. Slade will take care of things for you, while you sit in here and guzzle redeye," Hardrock returned airily.

"And listen to your till bell play a tune," said Crane. "All you do is waddle around and watch the dinero roll in."

"Can't see any rolling in because of all the free drinks I have to serve," retorted Hardrock. "Waiter! On the house! Strong

191

waters for the sheriff and Mr. Webb. Coffee for you, eh, Mr. Slade? And —"

"Yes, I'll have another glass of wine," Mary replied to his interrogative glance. "Oh, my poor complexion!"

"Looks okay, even at close range," Slade put in.

Mary wrinkled her pert nose at him as the waiter filled her glass with the golden wine of the Rio Grande Middle Valley grapes, which has no peer.

The banter was entertaining and amusing, but Slade was growing restless and he welcomed the suggestion Cruikshanks voiced a few minutes later.

"How about ambling over to my place for another one on the house? Come along, Hardrock, it'll sorta even things."

"Okay, for a little while," Hogan agreed.

Mary accepted with alacrity, Webb and the sheriff with less enthusiasm. In a group they headed for the door, Slade and the Hog Wallow owner bringing up the rear.

"Yes, I'm sure a heap beholden to you, Mr. Slade," Cruikshanks said. "I wouldn't have given a darn about the money, I'd have made it up to the feller and not missed it, but it would sure have hurt if something bad had happened to old Ben; he's like a brother to me. If there's any way I can even up, just name it."

"I feel the opportunity to do for those two devils evened the score," Slade replied.

Cruikshanks nodded, but didn't look too impressed.

It was a pleasant night and they walked slowly, Mary dropping back alongside Slade. Hogan and Cruikshanks began wrangling over the merits of various brands of whiskey. Webb and the sheriff discussed range affairs.

Without untoward incident they reached the Hog Wallow. A waiter escorted them to a big table not far from the door that led to the back room. Cruikshanks did the ordering after his guests had signified their preferences. The waiter hurried to deliver.

"I do like this place," Mary said. "Maybe it is rowdy, but I like it. Guess I'm just a hoyden at heart."

"I arrived at those conclusions some time ago," Slade replied, and was rewarded for his frankness with an indignant sniff.

"There you go, just like a woman," he protested. "I agree with you and you get your bristles up."

"You didn't have to be so emphatic about it," she retorted.

The Hog Wallow was noisy and gay, but not too crowded; folks were doubtless resting up in anticipation of the coming payday bust.

So the time passed pleasantly enough. The two saloon owners were still arguing brands. Finally Cruikshanks headed for the back room in quest of a bottle with which to illustrate his contention. He twisted the door knob, shook it, twisted it again. The door stayed shut. He turned with an angry bellow.

"Who the blinkin' blue blazes locked this door?" he demanded.

The bartenders looked blank. So did the floor man, and the waiters, shaking their heads.

"Well, it's locked," snorted Cruikshanks. "Fetch me a table and I'll bust it open."

Slade crossed from the table in three bounds. He shoved Cruikshanks aside.

"Stay in the clear," he snapped and hit the door with his shoulder, all his two-hundred muscular pounds behind it.

The door creaked, but stayed shut. Slade stepped back, and hit it again. And as it flew open with a crash there was a clang-jangling of breaking glass, and the back room was plunged in semi-darkness, through which he glimpsed two men flitting out the back door that led onto an unlighted alley.

He snapped a shot at them, knew he had

missed, plunged across the room to the door. And for the second time that day took a glorious header, landing with a thud on the soft earth of the alley. One of the Colts flew from his hand. He held onto the other. Flame streaked through the darkness and a bullet whined over his prostrate form. Half stunned by the shock of the fall, he blasted lead in the general direction of the flash until the hammer clicked on an empty shell. As he groped for his fallen gun, and didn't find it, to his ears, ringing with the boom of the reports, came a thud of hoofs dimming up the alley.

In the back room, boots were pounding the floor.

"Stay back!" he roared. "Rope across the door!"

There was another thud and the floor man was sprawled beside him, sputtering cuss words. The other halted at the door until somebody located and cut the rope, which was stretched from jamb to jamb, a little more than ankle-high. Mary Merril was first out, halting beside Slade, who had finally located his dropped Colt and was stuffing the cylinder of the other with fresh cartridges.

"Take it easy," he told her. "Everything under control. But if I don't stop turning flip-flops, I'll begin to think I'm a pinwheel."

"What in the world was it all about?" she asked.

"I think," Slade replied, "that Cruikshanks will find his safe open and the money brought from Comanche among the missing. Fortunately he wasn't snoozing in the back room, as he often is, or he would very likely also be among the missing."

Mary gave a little gasp and shuddered, her wide eyes peering apprehensively up the gloomy alley.

"Figure it was the pair that got away when you busted up the drygulching?" asked the sheriff, who had joined them.

"Who else?" Slade countered. "Yes, it was them, all right. Plenty of savvy and plenty of nerve. They evidently circled around and reached town unnoticed. Knew, of course, that the money would be in the safe. Got in by way of the back door, which was either unlocked, or they opened it with a duplicate key or a pair of long-nosed pliers, locked the door leading to the saloon, against possible interruption, found the safe door open or worked the combination. No trick for a hellion like the one we're up against. All the time they needed was a few minutes. Stretched that rope across the back door to foil pursuit, which it certainly did."

"And you figured it all out before you knocked that door open!" Cruikshanks, who had also joined them, marvelled in amazed admiration.

"Well, I thought it a mite funny that a door nobody would admit locking and which, I gather, never is locked, should be locked," Slade explained. "Decided a little investigation was in order. Guess it was."

"You're blasted well right it was," snorted the saloon owner. "But how you figured it all out in a split second that way is plumb beyond *me.*"

"Only I didn't figure in advance that rope across the door," Slade smiled. "That's where they were a jump ahead of me."

"Do you think you might have done for one of the devils?" Crane asked. "You sure threw enough lead at them; sounded like the war had started all over."

"Unlikely," Slade answered. "I was somewhat shaken by the fall and couldn't see anything to shoot at, so I just blazed away in their general direction. But I'm pretty sure I heard two horses hightailing. Fetch a lamp, somebody, and we'll go see."

The lamp was quickly procured. Slade took it and he and the sheriff led the way, Mary, Hardrock, old John and Cruikshanks accompanying them. The crowd, including

197

the help, who had streamed from the saloon, followed at a respectful distance.

However, a search of the alley for some distance discovered nothing:

"Reckon we might as well go back and finish our snorts," said Crane. "I'm feeling in need of one."

An examination of the safe, the door of which stood open, substantiated Slade's diagnosis; the money from Comanche was gone.

"To heck with it," said Cruikshanks. "Just so nobody got hurt is all that matters."

Slade smiled wryly as they sat down at the table once more.

"Might say the devil trumped my trick," he remarked to the sheriff. "He succeeded in tying on to what he was after."

"Uh-huh, but that pair we got laid out in the office ain't cutting in on it," reminded Crane. "I'd say you did a mite better than broke even. And when it comes to that, even losing a trick don't hafta mean losing the game. I know who's going to rake in the chips when the last hand is dealt."

"And that reminds me," said Cruikshanks, "I'm gonna fetch that bottle and show old horned toad Hardrock who wins the argument. Blasted door ain't locked now, that's sure for certain. Got a notion to leave it right as it is, busted and off the hinges. Nope, that wouldn't do. Then I'd never get a wink of shuteye."

"Never mind the bottle," Hardrock replied. "I concede. Plumb tired of arg'fyin'. And I vote that we call it a night. Tomorrow is another day, and it's liable to be a whizzer. What say?"

Nobody disagreed. Then, after calling goodnight to everybody and receiving a hearty response, they left the Hog Wallow.

EIGHTEEN

Shortly after noon the following day, Slade and the sheriff sat in the office beside the blanket covered bodies, waiting for the arrival of Doc Cooper and his coroner's jury. They discussed events of the night before.

Crane chuckled and cast an amused glance at Slade, who regarded him questioningly.

"Sam Cruikshanks was here a little while ago," the sheriff explained. "He had it all figured out that you saved him from getting his comeuppance."

"How was that?" Slade asked. "I don't get it."

"Well," said Crane, with another chuckle, "he said that if he hadn't ambled up to the

Branding Pen because he wanted to see you and thank you for saving old Holloway's hide, he would have been snoozin' in the back room and would have woke up with a knife in his back."

"Rather torturous, yes, decidedly round-about reasoning with a questionable conclusion," Slade replied.

"Uh-huh, but with more than a mite of truth in it," said the sheriff. "If he had been asleep in the back room when those two sidewinders crawled in, things would very likely have worked out the way he figured it. Anyhow, that's the way he feels, and he's plumb grateful. Guess he's all set to hand over the Hog Wallow to you, if you happen to hanker for it."

"I think I have headaches enough as it is without tying onto a few more," Slade said. "Nice of him, though, to feel that way about it."

"Said he would sure have hated to have a knife puncturing his hide, 'cause it would have leaked out all the likker," the sheriff concluded.

"I fear Mr. Cruikshanks has a macabre sense of humor," Slade commented.

"Guess so, whatever the devil that is," Crane agreed. "You had breakfast?"

"Not yet," Slade answered. "Decided to

wait until after the inquest."

"I ain't either," said the sheriff. "So after Doc finishes with his foolishment, we'll go eat before more hell of some sort busts loose. Here he comes now."

The inquest was brief, and on a par with the former ones. The coroner expressed a profane hope that he'd soon get a chance to sit on some more of the blankety-blanks. Slade and the sheriff headed for the Branding Pen in quest of much needed nourishment.

Business was already picking up. The Branding Pen was crowded with a jovial throng. Men were streaming through the railroad paycar and a steady increase of hoofbeats heralded new arrivals from the neighborhood spreads.

The Diamond F bunch rolled in, Bartlett leading. They shouted greetings to Slade and proceeded to do their bit to add to the general hilarity.

"Yep, it's going to be a big night," predicted the sheriff. "Here come Mary and old John."

"You look smug as a cat that's just lapped a saucer of cream and sees the door of the canary's cage open," he told the girl. "Must have had a good night's rest."

Mary refused to rise to his jibe. "I'm

hungry again," she said.

"Yet, you mean," snorted her uncle. "Well, anyhow you'll make some jigger a good wife; always meat on the table."

"I want some on it right now," Mary insisted. "Here comes Mr. Hogan; now I'll get some service."

They had an enjoyable breakfast together, after which Mary announced,

"I'm going back to the hotel to freshen up a little more. Didn't take time to make myself beautiful before breakfast; too hungry."

"You got by, in a dim light," Slade told her. Mary wrinkled her nose at the sheriff's chuckle and departed.

Webb joined some cronies at the bar. Slade and Crane sat smoking. Abruptly the sheriff stiffened and tugged his mustache.

Glen Graham had entered. He nodded politely and made his way to the bar. Slade was sure there was a derisive gleam in his keen eyes.

"Talk about somebody looking smug!" muttered the sheriff. "That blankety-blank!"

"Guess he has a right to feel complacent," Slade replied. "He put one over. Watch your expression, I'm still not quite sure how much he thinks we know about him. Best to keep him guessing, if possible."

"Right," said the sheriff. "Anyhow, he lost two more of his devils yesterday."

"Which didn't affect him in the least," Slade answered. "Their extinction meant nothing to him; just two less to divide the loot with. And don't forget, although his force is decimated, if he feels he wants replacements, he can get them. Plenty of that sort hereabouts."

"Figure there's a whole regiment in here right now," growled Crane.

"Hardly that bad, but some that will bear watching," Slade conceded.

"And that one in particular," said the sheriff. "Wouldn't be surprised if right now he's trying to figure a way to clean the Branding Pen safe."

However, Graham did not stay long. He had a couple of drinks and left without glancing toward the table.

"Now where's the hellion headed for?" wondered Crane.

"Probably to Tumulty's place," Slade guessed. "May have an appointment with some jiggers there, where he can discuss matters with them and attract no attention."

"Going to try and tail him?" Crane asked.

"I doubt that anything would be gained by it," Slade vetoed the suggestion. "He would assuredly catch on, and his sardonic sense of humor might prompt him to lead me on an absurd wild goose chase while his follower, or followers, got some work in. I'd planned to visit Tumulty's place, but I'll put it off for a while. Right now I'm going to take a walk. Tell Mary I'll be back before so very long."

"Okay," replied the sheriff, his eyes following, a trifle anxiously, his tall form out the door.

For quite a while, Slade strolled along crowded Main Street, nodding absently to greetings, for his thoughts were elsewhere, wrestling with the problem that confronted him. Where would Graham strike? Slade felt confident that the outlaw leader had something in mind. What and where? Slade didn't have the answers.

Reaching the southwestern edge of the town, from where there was a view to the west, he stood watching the glory of the sunset, shifting his glance from time to time toward the stupendous panorama of the southern mountains now clothed in flame and mystery.

Until the riot of color faded and the heavens became a vast blue-black vault in which the stars bloomed one by one, he remained, then turned and retraced his steps through the deepening dusk. He had enjoyed the walk but was no nearer a solution of his problem than when he started out.

Reaching Railroad Street, he made his way to Tumulty's place and entered. A glance around told him Graham was not present. He sat down at a small vacant table near the dance floor, knowing that Tumulty would join him.

The owner did, occupying the opposite chair. After a word of greeting, he announced,

"Graham was in a little while ago. Seemed quite chipper. Paid back the money he borrowed from the business. I told him to hang onto it and let the profits absorb it, which they eventually would have, but he said he'd rather have a clean slate."

Slade nodded, pondering the peculiar outlaw code of ethics. Graham apparently did not wish to defraud the man who befriended him, not thinking that the money he liquidated the debt with was obtained through robbery and murder. Something dubiously to his credit.

He chatted with Tumulty for a while, accepted a drink on the house and promised to be back later. He returned to the Branding Pen, where he found Mary, the sheriff and old John waiting for him.

"Couldn't find her, eh?" Mary remarked.

"Nope, didn't look in the right place until now," he replied cheerfully.

Mary glanced searchingly at the dance floor girls, but Slade grinned and refused to rise to the bait.

"Find anybody else?" Crane asked casually. Slade shook his head. The sheriff glowered about suspiciously and snorted.

Now the payday bust was really under way. The din was deafening, the smoke rolled in clouds. Everybody appeared to be talking at once. Nobody listened. Outside, the streets were about as bad, except there was less smoke.

"Blow up half the blasted town and nobody would notice," declared the sheriff.

"Wouldn't be much loss," growled Webb. "This one is worse than the last one. Fact is, they get worse right along, from my way of thinking."

"Perhaps it's just the crotchety disposition and the creaking joints of old age creeping up on you, Uncle John," Mary said sweetly, and was rewarded with an indignant denial.

"And I can still put any of these young squirts down for the count," he concluded. "They don't make men nowdays like they did when I was young."

"Now I know it's so," his niece replied.

"The surest sign of senility; 'When Pap was a boy' stuff."

Old John glared, but apparently concluded that silence was the wiser course. Which it probably was. Slade, listening with amusement to the exchange, wondered where Glen Graham was and what he was up to. He felt that if he continued to be unable to drop a loop on the elusive devil, *he* would end up doddering before his time. He experienced a growing irritation because of his lack of success.

A ruckus started at the bar, with fists and cuss words flying. A drink juggler whose cheek had been grazed by a thrown glass leaned across the bar and caressed a belligerent with a bung starter. Said belligerent lost interest in things for the moment.

The sheriff started to rise, but Slade shoved him back in his seat.

"Take it easy," he admonished. "They won't do one another any real harm, and Hardrock will soon have things under control."

Just the same, he never took his eyes off the row. He didn't think it was staged for some hidden purpose, but such things had happened.

Hardrock and his floor men waded in, flinging battlers right and left. The disputants drew back, glaring at each other. Hardrock ordered a round of drinks on the house and peace was restored. Slade relaxed in his chair. Just good clean payday fun.

"Well?" he said to Mary.

"I liked it," the girl replied, with a giggle. "Was exhilarating. But I'm glad you kept out of it. How'd you manage to do so?"

"It was a private fight, horning in would have been bad manners," Slade explained.

"Very considerate of you, it must have been a struggle," she replied dryly.

"Sure I'll dance with you," she told young Joyce Echols, one of the Cross W hands who had approached to suggest that they hoof it. "We'll leave these old fogies to their drinks and their reminiscences."

"Remi— remi— what?" stuttered Echols. "Sounds like some sort of newfangled chuck."

"Yes, the brand the aged batten on," said Mary. "Let's go!

"Be seeing you, grandpas, all three of you," she taunted over her shoulder.

The oldsters said uncomplimentary things. Slade laughed, and resumed wrestling with his problem. He was experiencing an uneasy presentiment, because he knew that Graham had paid off his debt to Tumulty, and that after one more good haul, the outlaw leader was going to pull out of the section. And he certainly did not wish to chase him all over Texas as he had others. He could do without that sort of unfinished business.

Deputy Estes and the two specials dropped in, reporting that all was peaceful as far as serious trouble was concerned.

"We heard there was a row here and figured we'd better have a look," Estes explained their appearance. "Blount is over at Tumulty's place, where there's an unusually big crowd."

Then Slade remembered that he had promised Tumulty to visit his place later.

So the ruckus in the Branding Pen, apparently innocuous and of no particular significance, indirectly was responsible for providing the opportunity Slade so sorely needed.

The deputies had a drink, chatted a while and then decided they'd better look around some more.

"And I'm going over to Tumulty's place for a little while," Slade told the sheriff. "If you don't mind, stay here in case I might want to get word to you for some reason or other."

"Okay," replied Crane. "This old coot and I will be right here. You be careful."

Slade promised to do so. Then he and Estes and the specials left together.

Outside, however, they separated, the deputies moseying toward upper Main Street, which appeared even busier. Slade headed for Railroad Street and Tumulty's place.

He was watchful as he walked the dark street. He did not believe that there was much danger of anything being attempted against him, as he felt that Graham had other things on his mind. And if he did pull out, he wouldn't bother his head about El Halcon any more. That is, unless the Ranger managed to catch up with him again, after he started operating in some other section.

Sauntering slowly, Slade passed the Hog Wallow, which was also doing plenty of business, but did not enter. A little later, he approached Tumulty's, which was undoubtedly booming. A little less than a block ahead were the lights of the railroad station. Otherwise, with its line of warehouses closed for the night, the street was dark, and deserted.

Slade entered the saloon, which was boisterous but peaceful enough and with no indications of trouble.

Tumulty came forward to greet him, smiling broadly, and gesticulating toward a small table near the dance floor.

"Kept it open for you, Mr. Slade, the one you like. Take a load off your feet and I'll send over a drink." He hurried off to perform the service himself.

Spotting Deputy Blount at the bar, Slade beckoned him. Blount at once joined him at the table.

"Sorta hoppin' here, so I thought I'd hang around a spell, especially as Tumulty said he expected you any minute," said the deputy. "How are things over town?"

"Everything under control, so far," Slade qualified his reply. "Estes and the specials are circulating and the sheriff is holding down a chair in the Branding Pen, keeping an eye on things there."

"Heard there was a shindig there," Blount observed.

"Just a friendly wrangle," Slade answered. "Blue eye or two and a few bloody noses. And one gent who got in the way of a bung starter the bartender was beating time to the music with, is nursing a mildly bruised head. Otherwise, nothing of importance."

Blount chuckled, appreciating the humor of the remark, and accepted with thanks the snort Tumulty placed before him.

Comfortably relaxed, he and Slade sat talking and sipping. And meanwhile, not far

211

off, things were happening.

NINETEEN

Once a week a money train rolled west from Laredo to El Paso, picking up the week's ticket sales at the way stations, and what freight money might be present. To and from Sanderson there was heavy passenger traffic. Also large freight receipts.

So the old safe in the passenger station packed a hefty sum of dinero.

The telegraph operator, who doubled as station master, was sitting comfortably at his table when a sound caused him to turn his head. He caught a glimpse of two masked men looming over him. Then a gun barrel crashed against his skull and he fell to the floor bleeding copiously. He was dazed by the blow but not quite unconscious, having enough sense left to lie perfectly still, as if completely knocked out. The only way he instinctively sensed he could hope to stay alive. And he was probably right.

From the corners of his nearly closed eyes, he saw the taller of the two men squat before the safe and twirl the combination knob as if he were perfectly familiar with the combination, which he probably was.

The robber took his time, working methodically with no show of haste. The door swung open. A locked inner drawer was forced with a small pinch bar. The contents of the safe were transferred to a canvas sack.

With a glance at the prone form of the operator, whom they did not molest further, to avoid unnecesssary noise, they left the station. The operator heard the clicking of fast hoofs on the nearby trail, fading into the east.

For a while the operator did not move. The devils might come back, or there might be others hanging around. Finally he staggered to his feet, having fairly well recovered his faculties, and went reeling up the street to Tumulty's saloon, the nearest place he could hope to obtain help.

When he entered and yammered forth what had happened, there was an uproar. Tumulty at once led him to the back room to have his injury cared for. Slade turned to Blount.

"Hightail to the Branding Pen and tell the sheriff to ride for Echo Canyon," he directed. "Tell him to ride fast but keep his eyes open. You ride with him."

Blount rushed out to care for the chore. Slade finished his drink, departed and raced to Shadow's stable, where he cinched up at top speed. Before he had quite finished, the sheriff, Blount, and old John Webb, who had insisted on coming along, bulged in.

"Mary wanted to come, but I wouldn't let her," said Webb as he flung the saddle on to the back of his cayuse.

"Right," Slade answered. "If it comes to a showdown, it'll be no place for a girl, no matter how nervy and able. Make the best time you can and there's just a chance you might catch up with the devils before they reach the canyon. Don't enter the canyon. If they happen to be in there, they would assuredly hear you coming and you'd be settin' quail. Wait at the south mouth of the canyon until I show up. Wait an hour and then if I don't, go ahead and learn why. Okay, hightail!"

The posse clattered east. Slade rode north until he was able to circle the north edge of the hills, then turned east, riding at top speed. He had a very good notion as to where Graham was headed. To his ranch house, doubtless to pick up money he had cached there. Then he and his remaining henchman would fade into the northern hills, where not even El Halcon would be able to trail them.

"Figure it's really going to be showdown," he told Shadow as the miles flowed back under the big black's flying hoofs. "If I can manage to intercept the devils at the north mouth of the canyon, the advantage of surprise will be with me. I have a feeling I can do it, that is if you'll stop snail-crawling and rattle your hocks a bit."

Shadow replied to the gross slander with an angry snort and fairly poured his long body over the ground.

Although the odds would be two to one against him and he would be facing utterly desperate men, Slade was fairly sanguine as to the outcome. That is if he managed to reach the north mouth of the canyon before his quarry. Anyhow, he welcomed the chance, being heartily sick of the days of uncertainty. Yes, he believed he could reach the canyon mouth first, although he was not certain. He had much the longer route to follow, and the outlaws would have travelled fast.

As he rode, from a cunningly concealed pocket in his broad leather belt he drew the famous silver star set on a silver circle, the honored badge of the Texas Rangers, and pinned it on his shirt front. The time for concealment, so far as the two outlaws were concerned, was past.

The miles flowed back. The great clock in the sky wheeled westward. A slice of moon rose in the east and the prairie was bathed in dim and ghostly light. Not bad shooting light, although it did render objects vague and illusory.

Now Slade was scanning landmarks that denoted the vicinity of grim and bloodstained Echo Canyon, the scene of many a deadly gun battle. Echo Canyon where the death cry rebounded from the towering walls of naked stone, and the thud of falling bodies.

Echo Canyon! The shortcut through the hills, and all too often the shortcut to Eternity. Slade rode on, expectantly.

Constantly his eyes swept the far reaches of the northern prairie. No speeding horsemen. There was no sign of life other than occasional clumps of grazing or sleeping cattle. Only the eerie cry of some night bird or the yipping of a coyote broke the great hush. Lonely and deserted was the rangeland. Slade's spirits rose. Looked very much like he had estimated correctly and would reach the canyon mouth before the outlaws emerged from it. Shadow, seeming to sense the urgency of even more speed, increased his already flying gait a little.

With nothing happening, they reached the yawning mouth of the sinister gorge, flashed past it to the east wall, for in the shadow of the towering east cliffs ran the trail. Slade pulled Shadow to a halt and dismounted, then eased him along a little farther and crowded him against the brush at the base of the slope that led to the crest of the wall.

"You should be safe enough here, loafer," he told the big black, bestowing an affectionate pat on the glossy neck now reeking with sweat. "Oh, all right, you can have a nibble or two, but don't move out into the light."

He flipped out the bit, loosened the cinches a trifle. Without comment, Shadow nosed a bunch of grass.

Meanwhile Slade was listening intently for the beat of hoofs on the stony trail inside the gorge that would herald the approach of the outlaws. Hearing nothing, he rolled a cigarette and moved forward until he was not far from the brush-fringed edge of the cliff, where he took up his post to wait, just out of the full glow of the moonlight. It was not possible to be wholly concealed, but he would be shadowy against the bristle of chaparral. Drawing deep drafts of smoke from his brain tablet, he waited.

Of course the sensible thing would be to mow the devils down the instant they showed, but he was a law enforcement officer, bound by the stern code of the

Rangers; he must give them the chance to surrender that he was sure they would not take. So be it. He still felt sure of the final results.

Abruptly, he straightened and pinched out the butt. To his keen ears had come a whisper of sound that gradually grew to the slow beat of hoofs. The outlaws, doubtless feeling secure against pursuit, were letting their horses take it easy, proceeding at little better than a walk. Which was all to the good from Slade's point of view. Tense, ready, he waited, hands close to his gun butts, stepping a little farther from the growth. Now the hoof beats were close.

Another moment and two mounted forms loomed at the mouth of the canyon. One was a slender, loosely formed man. The other was Glen Graham. Slade's voice rolled forth,

"Up! You're covered! In the name of the State of Texas, I arrest Glen Graham and other for robbery and murder! Anything you say —"

A storm of exclamations as the outlaws jerked to a halt and faced him. A grab for holsters, and the ball was open!

Back and forth streamed the lances of flame. Ducking, weaving, slithering, Slade shot with both hands. Bullets whined past

218

him. One ripped his sleeve, another tore through the crown of his much abused hat.

The slender man gave a choking cry and fell sideways, wrenching his horse's head around. The cayuse lunged forward, tried to turn, slammed into Graham's mount. Both horses went down, kicking and squealing. Graham was hurled from the saddle to strike the ground at the edge of the growth. Slade tried to line sights over the struggling horses, but before he could squeeze trigger, Graham dived into the brush and went crashing and crackling up the slope.

Slade rushed in pursuit. He had to dodge the horses that were trying to rise and lost precious seconds of time. Graham was still going up the slope toward the rimrock. Slade followed.

A flicker of flame as Graham fired over his shoulder. Slade shot at the flash, but Graham kept going, shooting again and again. It was a weird battle to the death amid the shrouding chaparral. Graham was definitely making for the crest of the slope. Why, Slade did not know, but he earnestly desired to overtake the outlaw leader before he reached the rimrock. The wily devil might well have a card up his sleeve. With Slade at his heels he burst through the final fringe onto the level space that edged the cliff top. Slade bounded forward, guns ready.

At the very lip of the rimrock stood Graham, halting to shoot it out with his pursuer. He lined sights.

Slade hurled himself to the ground and the slug passed over him. He shot with both hands.

Graham staggered, reeled back. Back another fatal step and, with a scream of terror, fell over the lip of the cliff. Slade held his breath until he heard the thud of his broken body on the rocks hundreds of feet below.

TWENTY

Slowly Slade rose to his feet, mechanically reloading his guns. He holstered them, walked to the edge of the cliff and peered into the shadowy depths. He could see nothing of the outlaw. Not that there was any need to. Glen Graham had paid his debts in full.

Feeling very weary, Slade made his way slowly down the slope. The horses had regained their footing and stood snorting indignantly. Slade glanced at the body of the slender outlaw, recognized him as the second of the pair that had intrigued him more than once. He passed into the canyon and paused beside Glen Graham's body. On the dead face, which was unmarred, there was, he thought, an expression of repose.

And as he gazed, a sound smote his ears, the clicking of fast hoofs coming from the south. He stepped back into the shadow to await possibly another onslaught.

But as the oncoming horsemen loomed before him, he recognized Sheriff Crane and the others and moved into view, slipping the Ranger badge back into its hiding place.

The posse jerked their mounts to a slithering standstill and volleyed questions. Slade pointed to Graham's body, motioned with his thumb toward the canyon mouth, where lay the last of the outlaw leader's followers.

"We heard the shootin' and came skalleyhootin'," explained the sheriff. "Not that we didn't figure you'd have everything under control. Figured maybe we'd get a chance to horn in on the fun. Well, guess the chore is finished, and maybe we'll have peace hereabouts for a change."

There really seemed nothing more to say, so they proceeded to load the bodies of the outlaws onto the horses they had ridden. In the saddle pouch of Graham's, they found the sack of money stolen from the railroad station safe. Riding slowly, in deference to their pretty well fagged mounts, they made their way through the canyon to the Sanderson trail and headed west.

"No, I have no idea why Graham was so anxious to make it up the slope to the rimrock," Slade replied to a question from Crane. "Perhaps he knew of some hidden way down the far side of the slope — he appeared thoroughly familiar with the area — or had in mind some place where he could hole up and have me at his mercy. Guess we'll never know for sure, for I'm certainly not in any mood to look for it."

"Anyhow you sure figured things plumb perfect," Crane said. "I can't understand how you did it."

"In a way, it was an example of the importance of seemingly unimportant little things," Slade explained. "Were it not for that fool fight in the Branding Pen, Glen Graham would now be in the northern hills, a free man."

"How in blazes is that?" wondered the sheriff. Slade smiled.

"Were it not for the fight, Estes and the specials would not have dropped into the Branding Pen and by remarking that Blount was in Tumulty's place, called to my mind that I had promised Tumulty to visit him later in the evening, which I'd plumb forgotten; I would not have been at his place when the robbery of the station was reported there by the station master. Would have been some time before we heard about it, which would have given Graham plenty of time to reach the hills and get in the clear."

"I see," said the sheriff, "but just the same it was an example of El Halcon thinking, and not missing any of the angles. I still can't figure how you do it."

Slade laughed and let it go at that, for he was too tired for any more discussion.

It was well past daylight when they reached Sanderson, to find that town very quiet, the aftermath of the payday bust. When they entered the Branding Pen in quest of a bite to eat, the bar was closed, the tables empty, with only a couple of swampers cleaning up, and the day kitchen help going on duty.

But seated at a table was a lonely little figure, waiting.

"So it's all finished," she remarked, after listening to a resume of the night's hectic happenings. "And I suppose you're off to the Post for more duty and more adventures. But not until you spend a week at the ranch house with us, resting up a bit.

"And remember what I told you before,"

she added, a smile twitching the corners of her red mouth, "if you stay away too long, I'll again come looking for you. And I'll find you, my dear, I'll find you!"

"Which is a plumb nice prospect to look forward to," Slade replied.

"Depends on what mood I'm in when I find you," Mary retorted. "All right, finish your breakfast and let's go home."

The employees of Thorndike Press hope you have enjoyed this Large Print book. All our Thorndike and Wheeler Large Print titles are designed for easy reading, and all our books are made to last. Other Thorndike Press Large Print books are available at your library, through selected bookstores, or directly from us.

For information about titles, please call:
    (800) 223-1244

or visit our Web site at:
    http://gale.cengage.com/thorndike

To share your comments, please write:
    Publisher
    Thorndike Press
    295 Kennedy Memorial Drive
    Waterville, ME 04901